KELLY'S QUEST

By

Buddy Ebsen

This book is a work of fiction. Places, events, and situations in this story are purely fictional. Any resemblance to actual persons, living or dead, is coincidental.

© 2003 by Buddy Ebsen. All rights reserved.

No part of this book may be reproduced, stored in a retrieval system, or transmitted by any means, electronic, mechanical, photocopying, recording, or otherwise, without written permission from the author.

ISBN: 0-7596-0328-6 (e-book)
ISBN: 1-5882-0187-2 (Paperback)
ISBN: 0-7596-0329-4 (Hardcover)

This book is printed on acid free paper.

1stBooks – rev. 02/19/03

Dedication

For their boundless patience, understanding, and belief, I am indebted without limit to two people, my soul mate Dorothy, and my teacher about novels, Darlene Jack.

Chapter One

Kelly watched them doing it on the bed. There were brief flashes of nakedness from beneath the cover, and panting, moaning sounds from the girl's parted lips. Occasionally they rolled over, spilling the sheet and revealing a full view of bare buttock. Then he was on top, more active. The girl's breath now heightened into accelerated gasps, crescendoed into a wild little cry of ecstasy. There was a pause followed by diminishing convulsions, a relaxed creeping smile and stillness.

"Cut and print."

Two "all clear" rings from sound.

The director, pudgy, bald pated, stubble bearded, wiped his fogged glasses as he and his camera operator straightened up from their kneeling position, bedside. Their proximity to the subject had compressed the focus range of the hand-held camera to its close-up limits.

"That's lunch! One hour for the cast, half hour for the crew!"

The A.D.'s announcement galvanized the set. Work lights popped on. Scene lights popped off as sound level on stage jumped with the general resumption of conversation and happy migration toward the door.

Kelly stood for a moment. She had watched the scene with the rest of the crew—the new ones, glassy eyed, drooling, the old hands yawning.

Copulation, she noted, even simulated, still packs substantial viewer appeal.

Kelly posed herself a question. Would she ever take her clothes off in public like that, and simulate this ultimately personal and properly private act of physical intimacy—for money?

Not on your cotton-picking life she told herself as the subliminal flash from her catechism hit her subconscious readout screen.

"As a jewel of gold in a swine's snout, so is a fair woman which is without discretion."

"Where the fuck is my bathrobe?" Superstar hunk, Brooks Rutherford's voice challenged the set.

Three assistants jumped. "Wardrobe! Where the hell is wardrobe?"

"Mister Rutherford's bathrobe! On the double!"

"Your car is waiting, Mister Rutherford."

"Your lunch is ready in your motor home, Mister Rutherford."

By the time Mister Rutherford's bathrobe arrived, his simulated sex partner had already slipped into hers and quietly departed.

While Rutherford donned his robe, Kelly noticed him consciously favoring the new script girl with a flash of his considerable physical endowments, enjoying her blush. There was no doubt that he "owned" the set, was aware of it, and let you know he was aware of it.

Kelly's Quest

To say that Brooks Rutherford's rating with his fellow workers was "lacks charm to a remarkable degree," would be flattery.

The crew privately dubbed him, "Our four million dollar asshole." But they knew his presence meant work - and you can't have it every way.

Hurriedly, the producer arrived, a revised script under arm. Martin Brice Junior, a slim young man with weasel eyes and a message: "Just saw yesterday's stuff, Brooks. Looks terrific."

Brooks grunted. "Yeah, so what else is new?"

"I'll run them for you," Brice cajoled. "You want to eat first?"

"I want a drink first. Let's go, Morgenstern."

Rutherford's command summons tore the director away from his hurried conference with the script girl.

As the three moved toward the door, Rutherford addressed his director. "Dave, did you ever hear of bad rushes?"

Morganstern, deadpanned, knew what was coming. "Not on my pictures."

Rutherford grumbled on. "You give the goddamn producers and cutters a string of Rembrandt's and what do they make out of them? Garbage. By God, I am not doing another picture ever, unless I get final cut. Are you listening, Marty baby?" He delivered this last into Brice's face, accenting it with a triple too heavy paw pat on the cheek.

Brice forced a grin. This was familiar small talk. His mind was on weightier matters. Time is money. A thirty-million-dollar picture and a ninety-day schedule. Each shooting day $441,178 goes out the window. Each hour, $55,147. If Rutherford now takes an extended lunch period, each extra minute costs $919.11. If the leading lady has to go to the john and she doesn't arrange to do it while they are lighting the set, it could cost $5,000 - six if she has problems - Ten?

The grab in Brice's gut warned him to stop thinking, settle down his stomach for lunch, so he wouldn't just be drinking Maalox.

They were almost to the door when it happened.

Had Kelly followed the crowd, gone directly to lunch without volunteering to help her brother move some lamps, it would never have happened.

Bending over to unplug a cable just as this top-level trio sauntered by, Kelly's well-formed, jeans-filling derriere became their focal point.

As they passed, the super star, with a smirk and a wink to his companions, dragged his hand lightly, caressingly, across Kelly's tempting bottom. They snickered.

Having played touch football with her brothers and their friends as far back as she could remember, when tackled by some fresh new kid and touch went to feel, it triggered instant response from Kelly, long remembered by previous recipients. Automatic, swinging from the floor, Kelly Ryan's leather-gloved fist caught Rutherford full on the mouth, knocking him off balance and backward into the arms of his producer.

Chapter Two

The beat of astonished silence following Kelly's reaction was broken when Rutherford spit out a tooth.

The producer reacted first. "Shit!" Brice screamed, lasering murderous fury at the dazed girl.

Shifting his leading man to his own feet, Brice slammed his script to the floor, stomped three raging steps forward, punctuating each with an escalating, "SHIT—SHIT—SHIT!"

Three steps back, he shook a trembling finger into Kelly's face. "Goddamn you! You're fired!"

Kelly started to say something that was going to be, "I'm sorry, but—"

He cut her off. "Do you know what you just did? What you just cost me?"

Again Kelly tried to speak.

"Get off the goddamn lot! Now!"

Brice whirled on the director. "Get a doctor."

Morgenstern echoed to the A.D. "Get a doctor —"

"And a dentist."

"And a dentist."

The A.D. picked up the phone.

Now shepherded toward the door, Rutherford alternately held his mouth and spit blood. His sole reaction since spitting the tooth had been a dazed passivity.

Kelly stood looking after them, tears welling. Slowly, she shook her head.

From behind her came a voice of doom.

"You hadn't ought to have done that, Sis."

It was Junior, her brother.

The "Junior" designation differentiated him from their father, but combined with his bulk, generated smiles.

Kelly whirled, eyes blazing. "Did you see what he did?"

His eyes on the departing trio, Junior ruefully shook his head, probably envisioning the monster shit storm that was inevitable. "Boy! When this hits the fan! They don't make umbrellas big enough to shield the Ryan family." Junior's voice was a gloomy tolling bell, programmed only to replay, "You hadn't ought to done that."

Pop Ryan was erupting. Had been for an hour.

The neighbors could track it audibly. Sometimes they shut their windows against the noise. When it was more interesting they turned off their TVs and listened.

Today's theme: I told you so, with embellishments.

Repeatedly, it emerged from the tempestuous torrent of orchestrated anger to be stated, restated, and stated again in the raw, jolting Ryan style characteristic of Pop during his fruitful years as business agent for the union.

"I told you, Kelly. But you bugged me and bugged me and bugged me. I told you there was no goddamn place for a woman in the Stagehands' Union! I told you it would lead to nothing but trouble, and boy, oh boy, did you ever prove I was right."

He paced a beat. "All my life I fought to preserve the union—keep it pure—keep out the blacks and unqualified bums storming at the gates to get on the gravy train. I fought to keep it a peaceful refuge where an honest working man could make a decent living, raise a decent family and later bring his sons in so they could do the same, like my father, Old Dan Ryan, did before me. Why, he founded the union for Chris' sake. Him and a few friends. He was lugging a shiny board up and down mountains for D. W. Griffith for coffee and cake money while the New York kikes was skimming the cream off the goddamn business." Pop paused for breath.

Kelly had heard it all before. She seized the opening. "Didn't the New York Jews start the goddamn business?"

Pop bristled. "Now wait a minute. Wait a minute. Don't change the subject. I'm talking about women in the union. I told you from the start it wouldn't work. But no, you knew better. You got a hold of that goddamn Washington Civil Rights lawyer bitch, or rather—." Pop's eyes brighten as he delivered this telling point, "She got a hold of you. Yeah, that's the way it was. They used you, Kelly. They crowbarred you into the union, her and that bunch of lefties and dungheads in Congress and the Supreme Court used you to spearhead an invasion into the sanctity of a pure honest union - to let the bars down. Now everybody gets in—niggers, wetbacks, more women. . . ."

It was Kelly's turn to bristle. "Wait a minute. Now you're changing the subject. I was sexually harassed, Pop. Remember?"

Pop snorted. "Harassed, my ass. If you hadn't been there, it wouldn't have happened. They'll say you waved your butt at the guy. That you asked for it. They'll claim entrapment."

Kelly stared. "What did you want me to do—turn the other cheek?"

Her comeback jolted Pop and momentarily propelled him into preposterous moral indignation. "That's vulgar," he pontificated, then continued, "Christ, I'm glad I'm not representing the union at the next bargaining session. They'll beat our brains out with this. 'Union member costs producer a billion dollars because she cold-cocks his prize ham.' They can sue us, you know. From now on, no Ryan will ever work in pictures again. What a friggin' mess." And so it went.

Pop's eruption, when it ran down, sent Kelly in retreat to her little backyard garden, her usual place of refuge when tension mounted. Her rosary, she called it.

Nurturing her roses and feeding her humming birds was nerve "damage control." It kept her sane. There she was joined by Queenie, her black neighbor, and sympathetic feminist.

Queenie had, of course, heard every word of Pop's tirade. After a furtive look toward the Ryan house, Queenie assumed her normal stance, draped comfortably over the board fence. From there she delivered her familiar message, "Don't you worry child, one day we are gonna take over, and we won't have to put up with this crap."

"We?" Kelly questioned.

"Us women. It's a comin' baby, believe me. They've messed it up. We're gonna heal it. All you gotta do is qualify. That's what my mama used to tell me over and over again. Don't protest! Qualify! And that's what we're doin'. Your roses lookin' good. What kind a food you given 'em?"

Later, when Kelly was alone, the events of the day very much on her mind, she tried to sort out what had happened. Obviously it was her fiery short-fused temper that always got her into trouble. A popular movie star drags his fingers caressingly across her bottom, a gesture a thousand girls might have welcomed, but not Kelly Ryan. She knocks his tooth out. Now she is out of a job, her two brothers probably out of jobs, and her father out of patience. "Why don't you think before you act, Kelly?" she reproved herself. But how do you do that?

"Kelly!" Pop would thunder. "Where in the hell did you get that stubborn streak in you?" Kelly often wondered what would happen if she retorted, "Look in the mirror."

The Ryan bungalow was a sample of affordable housing of the twenties that mushroomed on vacant Hollywood acreage to feed the demand of workers flocking to another California gold rush, the burgeoning new movie industry. The land on which it stood had been bought and subdivided in 1886 by a Kansas Prohibitionist named Harvey Wilcox. His wife Daeida liked the sound of it, so the place became Hollywood. This house had been her parents first and only home. Their children had been conceived, born, and raised there. Her mother had died there, and Pop was never going to move no matter how many "niggers" or "wet-backs" with triple family occupancy moved in next door. He would stay and fight them.

He was fortunate on the south side. The Jones' were, in his grudging judgment, "good blacks", which to him meant disciplined kids, a well-kept yard and no loud parties. Homer Jones, a fit 220 pounds in a L.A. police uniform was prepossessing. His outstanding record in football at UCLA, all Pac 10 tackle, carried respect. That Homer only wanted that and civility for himself, his wife, and his children allowed Pop to make an exception. He respected Homer, who looked him in the eye and wordlessly imparted this message. "We're all in this together. Let's make it work without unnecessary sweat." And Pop wordlessly complied. Though never close, eventually they were comfortable in each other's presence.

At six o'clock mass, the morning after getting fired from Cosmic Pictures, Kelly confessed her sins to young Father Hennesy.

"Was it a sin, Father," Kelly pleaded, "for me to react the way I did in protesting his invasion of my privacy?"

"No Kelly, not basically," Father Hennesy replied mildly in a voice flavored with the hint of a brogue. His manner told Kelly that she'd presented him with a puzzler. "But there are other considerations," he continued, "other people involved. The picture is shut down, workers laid off, some members of our own parish. Was it fair to them?" He paused.

Kelly felt his eyes studying her and thought she detected an inner smile. Finally he spoke.

"Kelly, you have not sinned. You have struck a blow against evil, but that was negative. Now you must do something positive. You must strike a blow for good. Listen to the next person who asks you for help. If his need is for good, help him."

Kelly had often heard the phrase "force majeure," but never knew its precise meaning. Since the picture had been shut down because of it, she looked it up. "Force majeure," an event or effect that cannot be reasonably anticipated or controlled." She thought about that. Yep, that was her alright. She read further, "An Act of God?"

Wow! Me, Kelly Ryan—an Act of God? Force majeure, while it staunched the dollar hemorrhaging for the studio, it simultaneously became one-day manna for the press.

The TV talk show comedians had a field day with it, and feminists cheered. Only one stuffy pundit, equating the situation with women in the military, expressed reservations.

Kelly went from church directly to Maybel's for breakfast. Maybel was an energetic fifty-six, heavy makeup on a once-pretty face. Thinning hair, currently orange, steel-rimmed glasses, immaculately clean, in a starched uniform. She moved tirelessly on legs remarkably free of varicosity, considering the work and the hours.

According to her oft-told story, Maybel had arrived twenty years ago from Kansas City—third runner-up for the honor of representing her state in the Miss America showdown in Atlantic City.

Convinced the judges were wrong or unduly influenced by private and sequestered interviews with higher scoring contestants, Maybel had been a sitting duck for a self-styled "Hollywood scout" who offered her a film test and a short cut to fame and fortune "in the movies."

"What that son-of-a-bitch put me through. I could tell you stories! Read my book. You want your eggs over, honey? Hash brown or fries?"

Superbly located just outside the studio back entrance, ample parking, thanks to an adjoining vacant lot, practically nestled up against the studio curtain wall, "Maybel's

Beanery" was a veritable toll gate for the ebb and flow of studio workers in their daily peregrinations to and from their jobs.

It was quiet this morning.

Kelly had debated whether to show her face in Maybel's, but force of habit won out. That and stubborn defiance. It wasn't her fault what had happened, and Maybel's breezy spirit lifted people to face the battle of each today. Besides, the place would probably be empty since the picture was shut down, so she wouldn't have to face the dark looks and leper treatment of some of her now idled co-workers. The beanery was empty except for two crewmembers seated across the service perimeter. They conversed in low tones with an occasional glance in Kelly's direction. She deliberately avoided eye contact with long stares into her coffee.

When the two grips got their check and rose to go, instead of moving directly toward the cash register they proceeded around the counter on a course that would take them past her.

Uh, oh. Kelly stiffened. Here it comes.

Kelly felt a tap on her shoulder, turned too quickly, and spilled her coffee. The men jumped back into exaggerated defensive stances.

When their eyes met Kelly's, they all laughed, joined by Maybel, who had caught the action. What had been tense, now was loose.

"Hang in there, kid," one of the men said, giving her a pat on the back. That was all that was said before the two moved toward the door. Kelly felt a surge of love for her fellow man, and woman too.

Maybel had demonstrated earlier a like support with a hurried pat on the hand and a "Heard all about it, honey. Don't let it get you down."

Suddenly, the world was a much warmer place.

Buddy Ebsen

Chapter Three

As the grips left Maybel's they passed a young man entering. He took a seat one stool away, laid two video tape cassettes on the counter and ordered coffee and toast.

Delivering Kelly's breakfast, Maybel's practiced eye read the young man's needs. "That'll never get you through the day. How about some ham and eggs? Got a special today. Buck ninety-nine."

He smiled. "On a diet." However, as Maybel left, he stole a quick hungry look at Kelly's plate.

Kelly's sidelong glance recorded him as not just handsome, he was beautiful, in the way that Robert Taylor had been beautiful, actually prettier than his leading ladies, though no less a man for it.

After a small smile acknowledging his presence, Kelly noted the cassettes. She read him for exactly what he was, a hopeful wannabe filmmaker. The town was crawling with them. She picked up one of the cassettes.

"What'cha got there?"

He grinned deprecatingly. "My masterpiece."

It bore a neatly typed label, from which she read, "Joey, Reel One, Written, Produced and Directed by Noel DeLacey," and the phone number.

"My." She smiled maternally. "Already a hyphenate. Don't you want anyone else to work?"

He laughed, "No one else in the class had time. They were all too busy on their own projects."

"S.C.?" she asked. He shook his head. "UCLA."

"So now," Kelly consulted the label to read his name, Noel DeLacey. "You are on your way to a meeting to sign with a distributor?"

"Heavens no!"

Again, the engaging smile and his soft southern accent.

"The last sequence is missing!"

"It was ruined at the lab?" Kelly suggested.

Noel shook his head. "It was never even shot."

"You ran out of film?"

"No. Equipment," he explained. "You see, I was shooting for commercial quality, way over budget." He picked up a cassette.

"These are just monitor I was shooting with 35. They told me my standards did not fit into a student film program. So they gave me a sort of premature graduation."

"You were kicked out?"

"No. They just told me my allotted time for the equipment use expired."

"So?"

"So, I scrounged. Used my own money, some my father had left me, to produce what's in these cans. As I said," again his depreciating grin, "my masterpiece, minus one scene."

Noel glanced toward the door and consulted his watch. "I was supposed to meet someone here who might be able to help me."

Kelly examined the second can.

Her mind screen was flashing Father Hennesy's admonition.

She studied Noel before speaking. It was a beautiful face, sensitive, and appealing.

"I'd like to look at this stuff."

Half hour later, through the courtesy of Kelly's friend, Edna, at Feature Film Service, a small postproduction outfit around the corner on Delongpre, Kelly and her new protégé were seated in a projection room watching Noel's film unreel.

The simple story was about the Martinez family coming apart through the normal attrition of modern everyday life. The father, a day laborer, the mother, cleaning woman, the children, Maria sixteen, Camilla fifteen, Manuel fourteen, Carlos twelve and Joey six. Camilla is unmarried but pregnant; Manuel sells dope; Carlos has just joined the gang as a runner.

The pluses are Maria, the eldest, who shoulders responsibility for the family, and Joey, the youngest, a charmer they all feel affection for. Life in the small Martinez home is a snake pit of contention.

One day Maria, walking home from the school bus stop, approaches the scene of an accident. As the ambulance drives away, a red blanket victim inside, she sees a mangled boy's bicycle in the street— Joey's!

Sympathetic police drive Maria and the bicycle to her home to report to the shocked family that Joey, the youngest, is dead.

They are unified by a single emotion, grief for the death of the youngest, an emotion the potential depth of which caught them all unaware.

Noel looked at Kelly.

"How do you like it so far?"

"Is that it?"

"No, the last scene is missing. You see, at the depth of the family's grief, Joey walks in."

Some kid had stolen his bike. His mother, who had prayed for a miracle, believes she has been granted one. She regards Joey like Jesus risen from the dead. She drops to her knees in thanks. It pulls the family together with hope for their future. "And all you need to finish your story is—?"

"A camera, a few lamps, and a small generator are all. I've got film—short ends. I can shoot it in a couple of hours."

"If his cause be for good, help him." The words of Father Hennesy formed an endless loop in Kelly's mind. Sure. Help him. But how?

The whirling cogs stopped on a name, Kevin, her kid brother. Kevin worked in the studio front office.

They met at Maybel's for coffee, and Kevin choked on a sweet roll when he heard Kelly's request.

"You, my studio-condemned and currently black-listed sister, are asking me to 'moonlight requisition' a truckload of studio goodies on behalf of some new-found little friend? To shoot God knows what. Are you crazy? No way!"

Kelly was not insensitive to the enormity of what she was asking, or the justification of Kevin's reaction; but this was, after all, to be a fulfillment of a penance, a theological matter, and Kevin just didn't seem to get the whole picture.

She was by definition, a "force majeure" — an Act of God. And the Lord moves in mysterious ways his wonders to perform. A recital of the underlying reasons, her confession, Father Hennesy's instructions, and Kelly's attempt at compliance got from Kevin, a blank stare. Honesty, in this case, was obviously not going to do the job.

So Kelly got real.

At last year's studio Wrap party for the picture, *Let's Do It*, Kevin got drunk and "did it" in a change room with cute wardrobe mistress, Mona Ferguson. In a moment of traded confidences, Mona had told Kelly. Kevin's wife, Irene, six months pregnant at the time, had not attended the party.

In her heart Kelly knew she would never rat on Kevin, but she also knew Kevin. He would never call her bluff. His silence, when she phoned him her threat, fed her gut feeling. He would comply.

The next day she reveled in the excitement, as she drove towards Santa Monica to check Noel's location. On a high, right with God and herself, and past mistakes behind her, she had never felt better in her life. Nothing could happen to spoil her day.

Where Bixel Street crosses 8th, just below the Harbor Freeway entrance, there is a dollop of abandoned space, the soil of which nurtures grass and a few uncultured bushes. This triangular scrap of land, left over by the City Planners, is afforded a measure of protective inaccessibility by the sheltering freeway abutment on one side and heavy flowing traffic on the other two.

Since nature tends to fill a vacuum, once discovered, this desirable building site quickly sprouted authentic California "packing crate" architecture and population to match.

As Kelly rolled along in her Jeep, she slowed for the intersection and became aware of a tall slim male figure standing on the curb next to the stop sign.

"Will work for food," read the escutcheon on his hand-held shield. The slouching figure was vaguely familiar.

"Duke?"

Recognition sent every cell in her body into reverse polarity. She rolled to a stop and made eye contact.

Yes, it was Duke all right. Haggard, unshaven unwashed, but . . . still the basically handsome face and features she had once adored. There still remained a faint resonance of the boyish charm that had stampeded her into that wild, crazy runaway to Las Vegas, a snap-on marriage and an aborted honeymoon. The once flowing blonde hair was matted, dirty, and the mouth she had kissed so many times, now ringed with crusted sores.

Her instant rewind and fast-forward took her through too many kaleidoscopic emotions too fast as guilt began to sneak in "Till death do us part." She felt dizzy- disoriented. Searching his sunken eyes, she queried, "Duke?"

His answer was delayed by a spate of deep chest coughs. It came with an apologetic half smile. "Hi."

Duke's helpless vulnerability choked her on a load of compassion.

Neither could think of a next line.

The car behind was getting antsy.

Kelly waved for them to pull around, but they preferred to sit on the horn.

Seizing her purse she frantically dug out a twenty.

Duke took the money automatically, wordlessly.

Reading his look and fearful he might false-pridefully fling it back at her, Kelly slipped her foot off the brake pedal and shot into traffic, narrowly missing a bus as she crossed the intersection.

Once on the freeway, distressed, dysfunctional, she almost hit two cars in a lane change.

She drove subconsciously, her mind churned memories. Was it only three years since they had left Hollywood at midnight in high spirits, headed for Las Vegas to get married? The sequence of events flashed back in high definition.

The four a.m. pit stop at State Line.

Dawn sneaking in from the East, while up ahead the glittering lights of Vegas still beckoned and stoked Kelly's impatient desires. Then she saw the hitchhikers. A beat-up young couple, tired drawn faces, pathetic baggage, thumbing their way toward Los Angeles. She felt a sting of fright.

Will that be us?

It wasn't too late to change course.

Should they really go on with this exciting craziness?

A quick glance at Duke's confident handsomeness had dispersed her doubts.

The wedding ceremony at the Graceland Chapel performed by the sleepy-eyed Elvis clone, his drab wife a witness, was a downer, but the bedroom scene following, thanks to Duke's know-how, had been a skyrocketing celebration.

He must have learned much from older women, Kelly divined, things like, "Never rush a virgin. Let her crave every next move before you supply it." As a result, Kelly had never felt any unconscious animus toward the man who took something from her that could never be replaced.

It was what happened afterward that derailed their romance.

Duke, with his infallible system worked out from a book entitled, *Numerical Probabilities*, had had astounding luck with the dice.

When he showed up later, cleaned out and shamefaced to dip into the 'case' money Kelly had stashed, she gave it to him. That he lost it too was not the greatest blow to their romantic idyll. It came when Kelly said, in jest, "Well, to get us home I can always sell my body."

When Duke seemed to consider it, Kelly experienced an instant of clairvoyance, a flash look into the future, which prompted her move.

She started for the door. "Hey, wait a minute," Duke began. "Where you going?"

Without stopping, Kelly flung back, "To hock my engagement ring for the gas money to get us home."

Duke's handsome face flushed in anger. "Goddamn you, Kelly, come back here!"

Kelly kept going.

What followed was the longest, silent ride in a car she was ever to experience. The chill of their romance was amply offset by the heat of her father's welcome.

Father O'Donnell engineered an annulment and Kelly lapsed into a period of penance, literally "scared straight." She prayed long and hard that the experience had not left her pregnant. When the answer to her prayers was verified by Dr. Mandell, the Ryan family physician, she promised God, in return, a faultless life of service.

Today Duke was a bum.

Did she feel guilty?

Guilty of what? Desertion? "You made me what I am today. I hope you're satisfied—over heart-rending violins." Kelly fought the grinning devils in her mind to dodge the implied guilt.

Duke was weak. A loser. He had those makings in him always, camouflaged with superficial charm. She had been too inexperienced to read his true character until Vegas, when her intuition had screamed, "Bail out!" She did. And she was glad she did.

No person, Kelly decided, can ward off another's destiny. Duke was history. Goodbye Duke. Goodbye forever. Before arriving at her destination, Kelly had pragmatically purged herself of every last smidgen of guilt. With this new project, her life seemed to have new direction with purpose.

However, that night she slept fitfully. There were so many loose ends. Would they all come together?

Buddy Ebsen

Chapter Four

The following day Kelly spent with Noel in frantic preparation for shooting.

Noel proved to be an efficient dynamo. Corralling his scattered cast took most of the day, leaving Kelly to worry. Would there be a hitch? Would Kevin deliver?

Her worries were groundless. At six p.m., the truck was waiting in Maybel's empty parking lot. The keys on the left front tire, loaded as per arrangement with Noel's complete shopping list—lights, camera, sound equipment, and the Mark III junior generator trailer hitched to the truck.

Good Kevin! Thorough, meticulous, trustworthy.

That night, at the location, Kelly watched as the pieces all came together. She particularly watched Noel, impressed by his expertise and control of his bright student crew.

"They turn 'em out sharp from the schools these days," she noted as Noel, completely in charge, rehearsed.

In his element, he seemed to know exactly what he wanted, and he got it without waste of time or motion.

She watched as he made magic with the materials allotted him. He controlled these unschooled actors with sensitivity, humor, and understanding to bring out of them performances they didn't know they had in them.

When the camera rolled, Noel leaned forward in his director's chair, reflecting every nuance with body English, chewing the corners of his handkerchief, tears streaming down his face at the emotional melding, the bringing together of Joey's disrupted family.

She felt the power of this simple manifestation of love Noel was capturing on film; suddenly she wanted to hug him and the whole human race. This was real!

She felt the fruition of Father Hennesy's intuitive direction. Something was happening here of far more importance than a copulation scene, and the winged spirit of rightness and elation filled her heart.

There was no warning except a barely perceptible light change, a slight diminution in the intensity of the set illumination that Kelly's practiced eye had caught. It came again. Closely followed by the student "juicer," she raced for the generator, parked out of earshot a half block away. By the time she got there, that machine had stopped running. It would not restart. She checked the fuel tank, then the oil dipstick. There was plenty of gas and oil. She had checked the electrical connections and was fiddling with the carburetor when Noel approached with a question.

"How long is it going to take, Kelly?"

Kelly, busy and miffed at his bland expectations of progress, muttered, "Who knows? A day, a week, a year." As he paced impatiently while she worked, Kelly raised her voice to a pronouncement level. "There is one thing you better learn and be ready for, young man. If you're going to stay alive in the picture business, it's never nothin'."

She continued to work with the carburetor.

Kelly's Quest

"The cast is losing concentration," Noel tactlessly continued. "After all, they're amateurs and mostly kids. If I only had some idea of how long."

Abruptly, Kelly stopped working and took a short stroll. She knew it wouldn't help to blow up in his face, and she knew she was approaching that point. A civil response to his bitching might have been, "With all due respect sir, that's not my problem," but Kelly was Irish. When she cooled down a little and traced the course of events that had gotten them to this point, she had to accept that what was transpiring here was her doing and responsibility. None of this would have happened if she had not made it happen.

Returning to the set, she found the younger Martinez kids fighting over the TV channels, Maria trying to do her homework, the father reading a Spanish newspaper, and the mother running the washing machine.

She saw Noel, emotionally drained, slumped in his Director's chair, his face in his hands, a picture of despair. Noel's student crew were standing around, still ready and willing but waiting for leadership.

Looking aloft at the service line running to the house from the utility pole, Kelly nursed an idea.

She had never done this before, but "Sparky" Kenyon, a garrulous old juicer, had once during a coffee break told her how to cut into a municipal power line.

He had told her exactly how it was done, how he had once saved a director's butt by this simple but somewhat dicey expedient.

Then Kelly went to work. In a miscellaneous spares box in the truck, she found two alligator clamps. These she joined to a pair of cables running to the junction box that fed the set lights. She surveyed the utility pole. It was the old wooden type with climbing studs that began twelve feet off the ground.

She backed the truck along side the pole. From the top of the cab, the rest of the climb was easy.

With the two cables, alligator clamps attached, looped over her shoulders, she climbed the pole.

When she arrived at the level of the service lines she found a small utility shelf. Taking advantage of it, she seated herself, drew a knife from her tool belt, and scraped insulation from the trunk lines. To these she attached the alligator clamps.

As she descended, Kelly saw the small sea of anxious faces monitoring her every move. This was live drama; the Martinez kids had even abandoned the television set. She slid down off the truck into eager arms and made her way to the junction box.

Now came the magic moment. Would her ploy work? Was the junction box now "hot?" The suspense was fully reflected in the faces of her watchers. Kelly picked up the cable feeding the key lamp and plugged it into the box. Instantly the set was bathed in light.

Kelly's audience cheered. She was spontaneously mobbed and hugged. Noel's approach was more reverent. He was awestruck. Tenderly lifting her hands, he repeatedly kissed them. Then he embraced her, murmuring, "Thank you, thank you, thank you."

Kelly's sense of well-being soared. It filled her with an exhilarating glow. For the first time in her life she felt exalted.

With the final scene in the can, there was jubilation on the set, a moment of celebration that was interrupted by a small "pop," a bright flash, and a shower of sparks from the top of the utility pole.

Simultaneously, the lights went out not only on Noel's set, but also in the entire neighborhood. At the Santa Monica Auditorium, a half-mile away, a rock concert in progress, guitars blasting, strobe lights flashing, blacked out. When the guitars went silent, the start of a historic riot among the fifty-dollar-a-ticket-holders kicked in.

Back at Noel's shooting location, two curious cops in a black and white had been drawn to the scene by the loom of the arc lights. Mystified by the blackout, they investigated.

The equipment truck plainly marked "Cosmic Pictures" seemed legitimate, but there was no traffic control officer, no unit manager with the necessary permits, particularly one granting permission to tap into a municipal utility power line.

Just this bunch of kids making a movie, possibly an illegal skin flick, in this Mexican family's house with no one particularly in charge except a girl named Kelly.

At the West L.A. Police precinct station, Pop Ryan, rendered by his daughter's new transgression a ticking bomb, bailed Kelly out then disappeared on what turned out to be a two-week drunk. Of course this happening, parlayed with her previous slugging of Brooks Rutherford, propelled the Kelly Ryan persona into a running character in an ongoing news story.

Noel's gain was more tangible. Instead of getting his first lesson in the heart breaks, vagaries, disappointments, illogical road blocks and fickle-fingered threads of fate, woven in recurring often idiotic design through the vast tapestry of show business, he garnered a press story that won the attention of an unlikely source.

Martin Brice, Junior, gambling hunch player, saw it in the *Hollywood Reporter* with a brief editorial comment. "Hollywood hierarchy would do well to check out the young crop of film creators. They will be the Hollywood hierarchy of tomorrow."

The story had created a small stampede of publicity-motivated Hollywood opportunists. Brice's interest came too late.

An alert talent hustler from top agency GTR had already obtained an option on Noel's creation, and so in the blink of an eye, Noel's fortunes seemed to soar and he knew the giddy euphoria of suddenly, from nowhere, being wanted.

On the dreaded day when Pop returned from wherever he had been, pale and hollow-eyed, he staged his inquisition. "Kelly," he began, "sit down, I want to talk to you." They were in the kitchen. Kelly found a chair and complied. Pop faced her across the table. He took a long pull from a half-empty can of Pabst Blue Ribbon and began.

"I've been doing a lot of thinking." He took another swallow of beer. He really did not need any more, but holding a beer can in his hand seemed to comfort and give him poise. "It was that goddamn war that did it."

Oh, Kelly figured, so this drunk wasn't because of her. It was in memory of his eldest, her brother Joe, lost in Vietnam. She had been through this many times, so she said, "Yes Pop," and settled back for a long sympathetic listen. "He was a broth of a lad."

Pop's eyes grew moist. "The finest—the best that was in Mary and me."

Though Kelly had heard it all before, each time it made her cry.

Kelly's Quest

"It killed your mother, poor Mary, frail little thing. She died of grief and a broken heart." Two large tears rolled unabashedly down Pop's cheeks. He brushed them away and took another swig of beer. "Mary left us just when we needed her."

Kelly agreed with that. She missed her mother.

Pop looked at his daughter with genuine fondness. "I raised you, Kelly, as best I could, with the boys. If you didn't turn out too well, it's partly my fault, but it's not too late to change things."

Change things! Red lights popped on in Kelly's mind. "Change what things, Pop?"

"You're a loose cannon, Kelly. Slamming around, knocking people's lives out of kilter. You've got to settle down girl, raise a family, find a steady young lad. There's still a few around in the union. You've still got looks, and with the annulment, you're still a virgin in the eyes of the church and you'll be much happier and we'll all be much happier when you—"

"Just one damn minute Pop," Kelly angrily broke in. "Before you start running my life for me, I've got a few things to say."

Mercurially, Pop's demeanor changed from benign to nasty. "You've got nothing to say. You hear me? Nothing! You wrecked the lives of what's left of this family. You got Junior fired and Kevin about to be fired from jobs I got for them and now you're driving me nuts." Pop rubbed his forehead as if that might drive away pain.

"I was doing God's work," Kelly bravely announced.

Pop's brow wrinkled in profound puzzlement. "You were what?" His jaw dropped in speechless amazement as Kelly continued.

"Force majeure. That's an act of God I was performing. I was doing something positive. It was Father Hennesy's penance."

Pop exploded. "What the hell are you talking about?"

"It was a penance," Kelly explained, "Father Hennesy imposed on me because of the trouble at the studio."

"Father Hennesy told you to steal equipment and blow out a municipal power line?"

"That's ridiculous. Of course not," Kelly protested.

"That's what you did, wasn't it?" Pop countered. "And now you want to blame the whole thing on Father Hennesy."

"No, I don't. You've got it all wrong. You don't understand."

Pop's rage dropped to pontification. "Listen girl. The church is in enough deep shit without you making waves. You say you were doing God's work. You ask me, it's the Devil's work you were doing, and that's what you ought to be doing penance for." He rose and took a brief pace, two steps one way, two steps back. "Well, this settles it. You and I are going to Mass in the morning, and we're going to thrash this whole thing out with Father Hennesy." Pop drained the last drops of beer from the can in his hand, crushed and slammed the empty into the trash. His way to the refrigerator was accompanied by dark mutterings, half to himself. "Force majeure! I'll give you force majeure— horse manure! That's what you're talking." He returned to the table with a fresh can of beer.

Kelly watched his progress as he opened the can. As he raised it to his mouth she spoke. "You drink too much."

Kelly's Quest

Her line froze Pop's action before the can touched his lips. When he spoke his voice was low and steely. "What did you say?"

Staring him in the eye, Kelly repeated her line. "I said you drink too much."

Pop lowered the can to the kitchen table. He stared down at it an instant. When the blow came it was hard and stinging, delivered with an open hand across the side of Kelly's head. Her father had never struck her before. The hit cued a beat of shrieking silence.

Under Kelly's wide-eyed, steady gaze, Pop instantly regretted his involuntary action. He started to say something, but Kelly stopped him.

Tears welling, she ran from the room. She sat for a long while on the broken-down sofa in a corner of her rose garden. A turmoil of widely disparate thoughts and fragments of thoughts raced through her mind, returning always to one reality: her father had struck her.

She thought of Mary, her sweet, docile, and forgiving mother, and wondered how many times he had struck her. She reviewed her situation. Junior was on location with a company in Texas. Kevin had an apartment.

What would life be like now, living alone in this house with her father?

Impossible, that's what it would be. Kelly heard the front door slam. Pop was out, probably on his way to Red's Hole in the Wall, the beer joint on La Brea.

She went to her room and packed. She couldn't take everything; just the bare necessities of wardrobe, plus personal things, notably her small white confirmation Bible, her Hollywood High class ring, a cross on a gold chain, some letters her mother had written to her one summer when she was away at camp.

She debated a moment about the silver framed picture of her brother Joe in his Marine uniform, then packed it among clothes in her two-suitor. Though Joe was Pop's eldest and most beloved, he was also Kelly's most beloved brother, and besides, she had bought the frame and paid for it with her own money.

At the bottom of a drawer Kelly emptied, she found an old forgotten treasure—a kazoo. It took her back to the romps with her family as they paraded around the kitchen table. Pop would sing in an assumed flannel-mouthed brogue.

> *"Oh the drums go bing*
> *And the cymbals ching*
> *And the horns, they blaze away.*
> *McCarthy blows the old bassoon*
> *While I the pipes do play. Hey—*
> *Hennessee Tennessee tootles the flute*
> *And the music is something grand,*
> *A credit to old Ireland is*
> *MacNamara's Band Ho, Ho, Ho*
> *Ho, Ho, Ho."*

On and on it went . . .

The memory was heart wrenching. She could not reconcile that father with the one who struck her. He had not changed without cause, she conceded. Joe, his first born, lost in Viet Nam; Mary, his beloved, dead of grief; now bedeviled by Kelly, the problem child.

Bugged by these extenuating thoughts, Kelly abruptly shut them out of her mind, dropped the kazoo into her two-suitor alongside Joe's picture, and prepared to depart.

Chapter Five

Where to go? Not many choices. She could pull some money from her Bank of America branch and go to a motel. Or—her face brightened with a thought.

"What about Marsha's?" Marsha Albright had been Kelly's best friend at Hollywood High. In those days, as now, girls hunted in pairs. Marsha, the flashy one, attracted the boys and got first pick. Kelly got the leavings.

This practice did not totally apply in Duke's case. Technically, without trying, Kelly took him away from Marsha. Marsha countered with shallow face-saving gamesmanship. "I was through with him anyway."

At any rate, over the passage of time, outwardly their friendship resumed structured on laughs over shared past experiences. Inwardly, Kelly felt there remained deep in Marsha's gut an unhealed scar, one small rankle, the kind no woman ever forgets. The filching of a boyfriend.

When last contacted, Marsha had a tiny apartment in Hollywood. Kelly had crashed there many times, bringing her own bedroll.

Dialing the number, Kelly got three rings and a recorded, throaty voice she recognized as Marsha's. "Hello. You have reached 213-749-7763. Please leave your name and number at the tone, and someone will return your call. Thank you."

Kelly did not wish to leave the Ryan number, then wait around and possibly encounter her father again when he came home drunk, so she responded, "This is Kelly Ryan. I'll call again later."

Before she could hang up a voice broke in. "Kelly?" There was warmth, surprise, and welcome in it, and Kelly welcomed that.

"Hi, Marsha," she said.

"Kelly Ryan, you little stinker. Where the hell have you been?"

"Getting into trouble."

"Yeah. Heard about it. Where are you?"

"Could we talk?" Kelly responded.

"Sure. Where are you?"

"At home, but I can't stay here. When can we talk?" There was a pause before Marsha's response.

"Write down this address, 1735 North Doheny."

"Wait a minute." Kelly feverishly fumbled for a pen. "OK." She tore a scrap off a newspaper. "1735 North Doheny?"

"Right. Strattford Arms. Can you get here in half an hour?"

Cued by Marsha's bluntness, Kelly gave her an out. "Listen Marsha, if it's inconvenient for you—"

Marsha cut her off. "Can you get here in half an hour?"

"Yes."

"See you then." Marsha hung up.

Kelly found the place, a posh new building in West Hollywood. She drove up to the entrance, her Jeep loaded with impedimenta, just as Marsha emerged in full evening attire and prepared to board a waiting chauffeur-driven Rolls. A single male passenger waited in the shadowy back seat.

"Kelly darling," she caroled. "So glad you made it." They warmly embraced. "The keys to my condo are at the desk. They have instructions to let you in. I've got to run. We'll talk later. Bye." And she departed in the Rolls.

There being no way to secure her luggage in the Jeep, Kelly carried it with her as she approached the desk.

The young clerk affably helped with her bags, let her inside Marsha's impressive condominium, and said, "Oh, that's alright," as he declined a tip.

After two incoming phone calls, it didn't take Kelly more than a casual look around to suspect her friend had considerably expanded the parameters of an activity euphemistically dubbed, "escort service."

The first she answered, the second she just listened to, cinched it. It also cinched her resolve to get out of this whorehouse ASAP.

That was awkward. After Marsha's demonstrated hospitality, she could not just leave; at least not until Marsha returned. But Marsha didn't come home that night. By midnight, Kelly, tired of looking at television, made a closer inspection of the premises.

There were three bedrooms. Choosing the one with the freshest sheets, she lay down on it, fully clothed, uneasy.

Early next morning, still alone in her luxurious surroundings, Kelly made coffee and picked up yesterday's *Hollywood Reporter*. Among the bits and pieces of news, rumors, and gossip, there was this item: "Unknown scores hit - GTR inks DeLacey."

Then it went on to say that due to interest from Latin American distributors and domestic art houses, this first film by an unknown could be, for DeLacey, the start of something big. Kelly felt two conflicting emotions. First, a sense of pride for having contributed to the discovery of this new talent and simultaneously a sense of being left out.

After a short internal debate, she decided to call Noel to congratulate him. That would be simple civility and could never, she decided, be interpreted as "sucking in" now that he was a success. She called Noel's previous number. No answer. Then she decided to call GTR. Surprisingly, it took a while to convince the female phone voice there was a Noel DeLacey on GTR's client list. Eventually, "the voice" found his name on a new list. Due to "policy," she would not reveal his number but would give him Kelly's.

At the considered negative of her name possibly going on telephonic records as one of Marsha's "girls," Kelly gave Marsha's number.

It was an hour before Noel called. He seemed ecstatic to hear from her. "Kelly!" His greeting was an explosion of exuberance. "I've been trying all morning to find you. Where are you?"

"Staying with a friend," Kelly answered hesitantly.

"I have so much to tell you and to talk about. I have got to see you. Can we do lunch?"

"Sure. I guess so. When?"

"Today. Are you free? I've got to see you!"

Kelly considered. "Alright."

"Meet me at the GTR office at one o'clock," he said. "Do you know where that is?"

"I'll find it."

Kelly's Quest

"One o'clock."

"Right."

"Kelly. This makes my day!" He hung up.

Kelly grinned. It is always nice to be wanted. She noted, with amusement, Noel had already picked up on the fact that in Hollywood you don't just "eat lunch" or "have lunch," you "do lunch."

Kelly's spirits soared. She dug her best slacks and a blouse from her hanging bag, found an electric iron among Marsha's things, and spent the next two hours making herself presentable.

At noon, Marsha had still not returned, so Kelly looked up the GTR address in the phone book, cranked up her Jeep, and started for her lunch date.

Noel's new business address, his brand new agent's office, occupied the entire seventh floor of a posh new building in West Hollywood. The lobby was a three-story hanging garden with a splashing waterfall. The elevator floors were maple. There was piped-in chamber music, and the main entrance portal bore in massive bronze letters the acronym GTR, of which everyone in Hollywood was aware meant Galactic Talent Representation.

Kelly's fingers closed on the bronze "G" that served as a doorknob. She pulled, and the solid carved mahogany door swung open admitting her to ankle-deep carpet.

The slim, beautiful brunette in basic black and a string of pearls sitting behind an antique desk raised her eyes. "Yes?"

Kelly smiled. "I'm Kelly Ryan. I have an appointment to meet—"

"Miss Cool" behind the desk, warmed with a gracious smile. "Ah yes, Mister DeLacey—I have a note for you."

"A note?" The balloon in Kelly's spirits lost altitude. The note read:

Dearest Kelly,

I don't know how to tell you this, but GTR has just succeeded in muscling Joey into the viewing program for World Wide Film Distributors convention in Las Vegas and forgot to tell me that I am scheduled to appear at the viewing at noon today.

Please understand and forgive, but this is the big break I have worked so hard for and that you made possible with your heroic help.

Should be back in three days with loads to talk about.

Love, Noel

Crushed, deflated, all dressed up, and no place to go, Kelly drove aimlessly for a time, gravitating toward water.

On Santa Monica Pier, she had a hot dog and sat for a long time looking at the sea.

Driving Wilshire east, she passed a movie house showing old film classics, stopped, bought a ticket and sat through two: *Casa Blanca* and *Breakfast at Tiffany's*.

Returning to Marsha's, Kelly found people there drinking champagne. After an effusive welcome, Kelly was presented to Marsha's guests. The introductions were first name only. There was Joy, a gorgeous young female with a pageboy bob, dressed in an enhancing simple black sheath, and Milburn, fiftyish, heavy timbered voice, hair sparse, a divot on top. The other male, Tommy, apparently

Milburn's friend, was an Asian who smiled a lot and smelled faintly of incense.

Milburn moved about the condo with an air of proprietorship, freely recharging his glass from the Möet Chandon in the silver ice bucket and spooning deeply from the mound of caviar in the Waterford crystal receptacle. After the introductions, Marsha disappeared to make some phone calls.

Kelly, not feeling at ease in this group, quietly retired to the bedroom she had occupied the previous night. Gathering her belongs, she prepared to depart.

Marsha found her there and, apprised of Kelly's intention, would not hear of it. "You're not fair, girl. We haven't had a chance to talk, and now you are cutting out on me. At least come have a bite of supper with us."

When Kelly pleaded dress code, Marsha whirled and thrust open a mirrored sliding door. She waved her arm expansively toward a cornucopia of plastic-shielded frocks, each with choice of shoes and matching accessories alongside. Then she pressed a button and her entire wardrobe selection began to move by on endless track. "There," Marcia said, "Take your pick, and don't give me crap about nothing to wear."

In the end, Kelly wore the clothes she had on, and since she truly could not plead previous engagement, she piled into a stretch limo with the gaily chattering group headed for "Jimmy's."

Their entrance into the bistro stopped conversations and turned heads. Jimmy, flanked by two captains, greeted and escorted them to their table, Milburn's booming voice acknowledging greetings along the way.

Once seated, drinks and food ordered, the parade of sycophants began its migration to Milburn's table.

For him, it made eating a temporarily neglected concern. Deal making came first.

Meanwhile, Kelly kept plugging away at her Alaskan king crab, smiling as she acknowledged the occasional perfunctory introduction. Actually she rather welcomed being ignored, because the cracked crab was excellent and she was hungry.

That's how it was until Jerry arrived. He was handsome and smooth, and though they were apparently on familiar terms, he did not linger to schmooze with Milburn but made directly for the empty chair next to Kelly.

"Hi," he said with a friendly grin. "I'm Jerry. And your name is?"

"Kelly," she said, giving him a neutral smile.

"Kelly?" he repeated. "That's a boy's name."

"I'm a girl," Kelly said.

Jerry laughed, gave her a quick appraisal, and answered soberly, "You certainly are."

The leveling quality of his tone and manner sent a warning flash through Kelly's man scope. *You are making an impression. Pay attention, girl. This guy could be Mister Right.*

She had caught Marsha's look across the table monitoring Jerry's approach and noted her smile of approval. However on second thought, that was disquieting.

"You work in pictures," was Jerry's confident assessment.

"I have," Kelly replied as she probed a crab claw with the little cocktail fork "Jimmy's" provided for that purpose.

"I've seen you in something."

He snapped his fingers, puzzling over which picture it had been.

Kelly smothered a grin.

"If you did, the cutter, the camera operator, and the director have by now all been fired."

Baffled, Jerry shrugged.

"I don't know what you mean."

"I'm a stage hand," Kelly said.

In the room noise, Jerry thought he had not heard correctly. "You're a what?"

"Stage hand, electrician, grip. I work behind the camera, not in front of it."

Jerry mulled this over. In the light of her femininity he was still not sure. "Did you say you were a stage hand?"

"Want to see my union card?"

Jerry studied her, then emitted a one-note blast of laughter. "You're kidding of course."

Kelly shook her head as she dug more meat from the crab claw.

Intrigued in a way he would never have dreamed he could be, by a girl–not just "a girl," a comely girl, a refreshing non-actress in a room crawling with wannabes–Jerry accepted Marsha's smiling welcome to her party.

When Milburn interrupted his wheeling and dealing long enough to finish his supper, Marsha signed the check. When they left, Jerry left with them.

The ride back to Marsha's was noisy and gay. Milburn and Jerry competed with remembered Jay Leno one liners that drew substantial giggles. Even Tommy, a little glassy-eyed from an overload of champagne, was impelled to venture a joke that was so unfunny everyone laughed.

Six in a limo was a squeeze. Seated together, Kelly was aware of Jerry's thigh pressing against hers. She also became aware of the scent he used. They made a chattering arrival at Marsha's. She signed off the driver and they proceeded to her condo.

An hour later, the other two couples having disappeared, Kelly and Jerry sank deeply into a cozy, gigantically cushioned piece of furniture serving as a sort of conversation pit, sipped champagne, and conversed.

Sometimes, Kelly observed, as in the lottery-ball mix of human entities, two people meet, and, cued by rapport, are impelled to pour out to each other in this brief encounter intimate, long-lost details of their lives they would never have revealed to old friends. A champagne buzz tends to enhance this state.

Kelly and Jerry talked about their origins, their marriages, his two, her one, and their families.

"My old man was a lush," Jerry related. "He used to come home drunk and beat me."

Kelly smiled sardonically. "So what else is new?"

"I left home," Jerry continued, "after my mother died. Ran away, lied about my age, and did a hitch in the Navy. Took one of their correspondence courses to prepare myself for civilian life. I chose accounting."

"Sounds boring," Kelly said.

"To some people it is," Jerry agreed. "Just numbers on a piece of paper. But if you read the numbers right, they can be exciting."

"Like Bingo?"

Kelly's Quest

"Better," Jerry said with a confident grin.

Kelly liked his mouth. She studied the way his lips moved when he talked. They sort of preformed the words as they came out, a little to one side.

"After I mustered out, I got a job in Washington in the General Accounting Office. It was just a routine job until all those building and loans went sour and the government had to take them over."

"I remember," Kelly said. "My parents lost money in one."

"I was one of the guys assigned to run the numbers on them. Most were disasters, but there were some not as broke as people thought. Then one night in a bar, I met a guy with money, the smarts and connections."

As Kelly listened, she became increasingly aware of the scent he used. It excited her.

"We made a deal," Jerry continued. "I bird-dogged the goodies, he stole them, reorganized, and resold them. We split the profits. Today he's a billionaire. I'm not yet, but I've got so much money I have to hire accountants to keep track of it for me."

Kelly grinned. "Aw, poor baby."

Jerry laughed. "I didn't mean to bore you."

"You don't," Kelly said.

She sipped some wine and pondered the seductive charm of rich personable men. Kelly set her glass down and stretched languorously.

Jerry studied her.

They were close, shoulders touching in this voluptuously upholstered loveseat. Slowly and deliberately he set his glass down on the end table next to hers. Sliding his arm around her unresisting body, he drew her close and planted a kiss on her mouth.

Kelly gave no resistance. Her conscious self wondered about that. Her thoughts seemed to be coming from a position outside her body, from which she could look down and observe the scene objectively. What she saw was Kelly returning Jerry's rising passion, kiss for kiss. Kelly abruptly disengaged herself and rose to her feet.

Jerry scrambled up and confronted her. "Something I said or did?"

Kelly smiled and shook her head. "Just want to check the facilities."

Jerry grinned. "Oh."

As she moved away, weaving slightly, he sotto-voce caroled after her in honey dripping tones, "Don't keep me waiting."

Kelly turned, smiled, and caroled back, "Don't be pushy."

Five minutes later, while Kelly was leaving the bathroom, she encountered Marsha entering.

Marsha, attired only in pajama top and smiling delightedly, gave Kelly a big happy thumb-and-forefinger okay sign. "Nice going. Your guy, Jerry, obviously likes you. He's a gilt-edged, thousand-dollar customer, and since I like you, Kelly girl, there'll be no forty-percent commission. I'll handle the business details. Hasta la vista – Ciao." She gave Kelly a hug and was back out the door.

Kelly, suddenly cold sober, looked at herself a long time in the mirror. Marsha's naked cash reference had flagged a warning. She was being marked down to Marsha's level. It was a mixed feeling, born, Kelly surmised, of Marsha's need to validate her own values by eroding Kelly's. It was certainly no favor Marsha was offering, but in a way, a reverse payback for what had happened at Hollywood High with Duke years before. In sum, it said, "Come on Kelly, get off it – we're all whores. It just depends on how high they stack the money." Marsha had put the ball squarely in her court.

The next call was totally Kelly's.

Buddy Ebsen

Chapter Six

Jerry had disappeared. He waited for her, she presumed, in the third bedroom. Kelly sneaked her bag and bedroll out the front door. There was a chill in the night air. But it smelled good—fresh and clean as she wiped the dew from her windshield:

'Get out of town, before it's too late.

Get out of town, be kind to me please.'

Cole Porter's lyric, though not a perfect fit for her present situation, kept running through Kelly's head.

Quarter to two in the morning is not a prudent time to be withdrawing cash from an automatic teller anywhere in the current American scene, particularly in steel-shuttered-store fronted Hollywood.

Aware of that danger, Kelly drove up close and left the motor running. After a careful look around, she got out and approached the money dispenser. Inserting the card, she punched her numbers and was seated in the jeep counting her twenties, when from nowhere a car materialized, blocking her exit.

Terrified, she slammed into reverse, tires shrieking as the spinning wheels dug her out of the trap. A metal-testing gearshift – jump forward – sharp right – a bump over the curb and out of the lot, spinning wheels flinging back gravel. She was long gone before those two in the car could follow. In their attempt, they grounded on the curb.

A "staked out" black and white rolled in from the shadows, blocking their further progress. The stalwart LAPD took charge.

Kelly, by now out of sight, spotted no pursuers. She began to relax and consider where she was going. There was much of the world she had never seen. This unsolicited opportunity having been thrust upon her, why not take advantage of it.

She had two hundred dollars in cash, a Visa, a Standard gas card, and an eighteen hundred sixty-seven dollar reserve in her account. She had always wanted to drive north on 101 with no particular destination.

In the Sunday *L.A. Times* travel section, there were beckoning stories about the wine country, the mother-lode country, and the picturesque coastline above Mendocino. Why not see some of these places? She had promised that to herself "someday." Well, through an unscheduled set of circumstances, she decided—"Today is someday!"

She started driving north on US 101. Having become familiar with Solvang and Santa Barbara in previous years, Kelly decided to avoid these stops and target her explorations on the Great Northwest. Once she made these decisions, she thrust her worries aside and plunged into the new adventure with zestful excitement.

Predawn, traffic light, she made San Luis Obispo by 7:00 a.m. She checked into a motel, slept soundly, and woke up hungry. It was three in the afternoon. A hearty breakfast of ham and eggs, hash browns and some particularly good coffee at the adjoining coffee shop, fortified her for the next leg of her trip.

Kelly's Quest

By driving until midnight and skirting cities, she made it to Eureka, where she found a vacancy in a seaside motel.

Lulled by the surf, she again slept soundly, awakened at dawn by a mood change in the sea. It still wore a windless morning slick, but out of the mist shrouded horizon came huge oily China-born rollers that crested and exploded into murmuring beach-bound surf. As she sat up in bed, Kelly could see the beach. Sea gulls stood on the sand in small sullen groups, waiting for sun and breeze to provide a thermal.

Lying back to luxuriate on a comfortable mattress, dozing on and off, Kelly was surprised to discover it was 10:30. She rose, showered, dressed leisurely, and during an exploratory walk discovered an eating-place of weathered beach-shack architecture with a fishnet, shell, and glass-net float decor.

The special was fresh caught white sea bass, a glass of Mondavi, and all the bread you want to feed the Sea gulls, $2.75. Kelly went in.

Later, spirits warmed by the wine and the afternoon sun, she tossed crusts of bread to the sea gulls, now airborne, who caught them on the wing. She felt completely at peace here, doing just that, not wanting to be elsewhere, doing any other thing. Hollywood was a faraway place—on another planet.

More sea gulls arrived, attracted by the handout. Kelly got a refill on the bread to feed the newcomers.

Lucky gulls, she mused. They had it made. Nobody was tossing Kelly any bread. She had to scratch for it.

Her dreamy state invaded by reality, some of the light began to leak out of her adventure. She wondered where her next job was coming from. Outside of Hollywood, there were very few opportunities for a currently blacklisted studio electrician. Inside Hollywood, there were none.

The next day it rained. She made Tacoma by nightfall. Traffic was heavier on the approaches to Seattle. Compounded by rain, it dampened Kelly's spirits. The more attractive motels bore "no vacancy" signals. When she finally found a vacancy, she shared it with roaches. The hot water wasn't. The toilet kept running, and the rain kept raining.

With the rain came loneliness and memories of her mother's funeral. As always, they made Kelly quietly cry. Her tears matched the raindrops on the windowpane. She tried to sleep, but the night brought a sense of rootless strange-town blues, a scariness that made her yearn for familiar places.

It also caused her to count her money twice.

Usually one to shrug off mischance with a buoyant, 'Win a few, lose a few,' Kelly discovered her present threshold of tolerance was running low. She thought it over. Her plans were not set in concrete. She could always go back, or change course and look for better weather.

It was still raining when early the next morning Kelly left Tacoma, on State 18 to US 90, and headed east.

As she crossed the Bitter Root Range in northern Idaho the weather cleared and the terrain changed character. The picturesque mountains that stirred Kelly rekindled a zest for adventure.

This was the real west of cowboys and Indians and rocky mountain grizzly bears, the west of a thousand story books and motion pictures that comes to mind when people speak or write of "THE WEST" in capital letters.

Kelly's Quest

Where 90 crosses the Idaho-Montana line, Kelly passed a sign reading, "Paradise 13 miles."

Intrigued, she rolled to a stop, considered, and then backed up to a sign marked "Scenic Route," which crossed the main highway. Smiling inwardly, she unlimbered her camera, placed it on the hood, set "delayed shutter," and let it snap a picture of herself next to the sign, thumbing a ride.

If she never made it to Paradise, she chuckled, at least she could show friends how close she had come. While parked there, three cars and a pickup turned off and disappeared up the side road. Curious, Kelly followed. A mile on her way, she came to a sign labeled, "Showlo," marking the outskirts of a small settlement. The most imposing building was a large log slab styled establishment. It bore a garish neon sign heralding the message "Jack Slade's State Line Corral Cafe Casino," the last three words cleverly utilized a single, jumbo C.

The parking lot was choked with vehicles. There was a filling station. Kelly drove in.

As the young Indian attendant filled her gas tank and checked the oil, Kelly looked around. She became aware of a face at a window in the adjoining building. Someone was watching.

When she gave the Indian her credit card, the watcher emerged from the door marked "office," took her card from the boy and approached. He was tall, dark, handsome, and over-confident. "Howdy ma'am. I'm Jack Slade. This is my place, and I always like to personally welcome new customers, especially if they're beautiful."

Kelly gave him a nod and a perfunctory smile.

"Tonto," Slade reprimanded the Indian. "Clean the bugs off the lady's windshield, will you?"

As the boy moved to comply, Slade proceeded with the paper work. "Hollywood California. You're a very long way from home. Where you headed?"

"East."

"What's your hurry, sweetheart? Park this thing. We've got a happy hour going in fifteen minutes. Party time!" He gave her a small insinuating leer.

Kelly had scoped this guy on sight, and her readout screen had already flashed, *No way!* Kelly signed, took the receipt, and her card.

Slade persisted. "How about it?"

"Thanks, but no thanks. Got to run."

"You're meeting somebody?"

"How'd you guess?" She hit the starter button. As she rolled away, the novelty plate bolted to the Jeep rear bumper revealed its message. "Not For Hire."

Slade's eyes locked on it, and he grinned.

Eyeing him in the rearview mirror, Kelly quietly summarized the encounter. "And as far as you are concerned, mister—that is not a come on."

Chapter Seven

The blue-as-paint sky hung like a canopy over a washed world. Five miles down the road, through broad sweeping range country rimmed by soul-cleansing vistas of distant white-tipped mountains, the jeep coughed twice and quit. Kelly put it in neutral and hit the starter button. It started and ran intermittently until it stopped for good.

Kelly got out, raised the hood, disconnected the fuel line, and blew through it. She had not had time to notice two riders and a dog rounding up strays on the nearby range. They had noticed her but had not let it interrupt their work.

The last recalcitrant calf finally secured in the crude range holding pen, one rider loped a little closer, stopped, and watched Kelly work.

She became vaguely aware of him as she got in and turned the engine over. It roared, hopefully alive for five seconds, then it coughed twice and died. When she turned it over, the abused battery cranked the starter without success until it quit.

This development cued the watching horseman to start his mount walking toward the stalled Jeep.

Kelly, fully aware of his approach, was still trying to coax life out of her battery, when his voice interrupted. "Sounds like you've got a dead battery, ma'am."

To this redundant appraisal of the obvious, Kelly was tempted to respond with a line that eloquently expressed her present exasperation, something smart-ass like, "no shit?" But after looking him over, she changed her mind and laconically delivered an ironic, "yup," with mischievous Gary Cooper overtones.

Like a good painting that registers at the instant of first view a totality of effect, so did the visual elements that made up this cowboy's persona impact with compelling positive unity on Kelly Ryan. Chiseled bronze features, clear blue eyes with the look of eagles about them; from his weathered, authentically shaped sweat-stained Stetson to his dusty, honestly-aged spurred boots, the tall, lean, hard-muscled body in between, he was the veritable Marlboro Man!

They must be shooting the commercial somewhere close by, Kelly mused, and this guy has wandered off the set. Any minute the AD will come charging over the rise—looking for him.

The rider dismounted and stepped over to the open hood. He looked in. "Gas line's plugged," Kelly volunteered. He looked up and around. His helper and the dog apparently had the drover situation in hand. He shut the hood, uncoiled two lariats from his saddle and rigged them, one to each end of the Jeep's front bumper, then around his horse's chest over the leather breast strap securing the end around his saddle horn. Remounted, he turned to Kelly. "Put her in neutral," he ordered, "and take the brake off."

She complied.

Subtly pressing the "go-ahead button" on his horse, they started forward and proceeded to roll down the long easy grade.

Manning the steering wheel, Kelly expressed her natural curiosity. "Where are we going?"

He turned in his saddle as the horse plodded along, looked at her a beat before answering, "My place." Then he turned away as they continued to roll.

A sugar rush of dangerous excitement swept Kelly. Way down deep she had always been looking for a "take-charge guy," but here she was, a girl alone on the road with broken down wheels. A stranger rides up, lassos her Jeep, and proceeds to haul it and her off to "his place" after no more introduction than three lines of dialogue, and she lets him!

This is crazy. *What's come over you, girl?* What could it lead to? But as she looked at his broad shoulders, slim hips, straight back and easy motion in the saddle, she began to think outrageous thoughts. With a man like this, "a fate worse than death" could be suffering from a bad rap.

They turned off the road and passed a sturdy pair of gateposts supporting a crossbeam from which hung a jumbo version of a branding iron. It was composed of three horseshoes and a piece of pipe neatly welded together to say 'JB.'

Leaving the road, they rolled a quarter mile down a lane toward a small clump of cottonwoods. Halfway to the ranch house, now revealed by its lighted windows in the gathering dusk, three border collies raced out to announce their coming.

As they rolled to a stop in the wide yard area, Kelly became aware of a woman standing in the doorway, watching. She took a step onto the veranda. The light illuminated her "Margie Main" type face. There came a breezy exchange between Kelly's captor and the woman she correctly assumed to be his mother. "Alright, cowboy, what kind of stray you got roped this time?"

"Don't know yet. No brand on her."

Kelly smiled with a sense of warm comfort at this laconic, disarming dialogue. Nevertheless, somewhat apprehensive at the women's deadpan scrutiny, Kelly ventured an apology. "Sorry about the intrusion, ma'am, I didn't have a choice." Kelly opened the door and slid out of her vehicle.

"Yeah. So I see," the woman responded as she watched the removal of the two lariats from the Jeep's bumper. "He had two ropes on you." She turned to look poker-faced at Kelly, who knew she was being sized up. "I'm Marge Hunnicutt." The woman stuck out her hand. "Welcome to the JB Ranch."

As they shook, Kelly responded. "Kelly Ryan. I hope I'm not intruding."

Marge Hunnicutt overrode Kelly's attempted apology. "You're just in time for supper. Gary will bring your stuff. Come on in." Leading the way, she started for the ranch house.

While her son occupied himself with horse barn matters, Marge Hunnicutt played hostess. Kelly was led to the guestroom of the simple, rugged one-story dwelling. The way was through an expansive living area, dominated by a massive fieldstone fireplace, studded with hooks from which hung a huge iron stew kettle, and various iron cooking utensils that spoke of practical use during earlier times.

Where not native fieldstone, the walls were of rough-sawn, undressed lumber that made for a primitive ruggedness that Kelly found pleasing. The walls were decorated with woven sheep's wool Indian blankets, and one cougar skin, snarling jaws intact. Several wall niches supported colorfully painted Indian pottery. An antlered deer head poked into the room above the fireplace, and a stuffed eagle, wings spread, soared on a wire from the ceiling.

The guest bedroom was Spartan; two double-decked bunks and a chest of drawers. There was one bathroom. It housed a vintage iron bathtub on legs and a washbasin. The toilet, also a period piece, was flushed from a tank on the wall above it, activated by a dangling chain pull. Regardless of its antiquity, all the plumbing worked.

Refreshed, Kelly joined her hostess in the kitchen where, despite the presence of a wood-burning stove, a pot of stew was bubbling on a gas range.

"Please don't go to any extra trouble for me, Mrs. Hunnicutt," Kelly began. "What can I do to help?"

"Just sit down, child," Marge Hunnicutt responded, "and the name is Marge, even to my son. The last person to call me Mrs. Hunnicutt was my husband, and that was only when he was mad at me." As she spoke, she ladled out a bowl of the steaming hot stew. "How far did you drive today?"

"From Tacoma," Kelly said, as she sat down and sniffed the aroma. "Gee, this smells good, but shouldn't we wait for your son? And how about you?"

"No," Marge shook her head. "I already ate, and there's no telling when he'll show up, once he gets going down at the barn. Always something got to be done. You run a ranch, you're never gonna get caught up. Eat, child, 'fore it gets cold!"

"Home baked," she said as she placed a platter of sliced bread on the table.

Kelly tasted the stew. "This is absolutely delicious!"

"Should be," was Marge's laconic reply. "Been practicing about fifty years. So, you drove all the way from Tacoma, did you?"

"Yes, ma'am, through beautiful country," Kelly replied.

"I noticed you had California plates."

"Yes, I'm from Hollywood," Kelly said.

Marge's eyes widened. "Hollywood? California? Really? You work in the movies? You're an actress?"

"No." Kelly took a mouth full of stew and shook her head. "I'm a stagehand." Then responded to Marge's blank look, "An electrician."

Marge looked doubtful.

"A stagehand? A pretty girl like you? That's a man's work."

Kelly shook her head. "Not exclusively. Not any more."

Marge picked up and examined Kelly's idle hand. "No calluses."

Kelly grinned. "I wear leather gloves and use a lot of Jergen's lotion."

Marge studied the short unpolished nails, sniffed and shook her head. "A stagehand - well, why not?" She gave Kelly back her hand and a long reflective look that made Kelly feel she was being X-rayed.

After the revitalizing bowl of mulligan stew and a hot bath, Kelly lay in Marge's guestroom bunk bed and reviewed the day's events. Miraculously, she had arrived at a place where she had an instant sense of belonging, of "fitting in" to a void that seemed to be there, waiting for her.

When she had almost discarded her belief there was such a place for her in this world, here it was. But this was insane. How could that be? How could it have been planned? She must be overtired - fantasizing.

Between spells of dozing off, she made a mental note, these were good people. She must not impose on their hospitality.

Buddy Ebsen

Chapter Eight

Awake at dawn, Kelly heard activity in the kitchen.

Guilty at the thought of being judged a city-bred slugabed, she dressed hurriedly and made for the kitchen. There was a pot of hot coffee on the stove and steak broiling in the oven, but no people.

She poured herself a cup of coffee and stepped out the kitchen door to a veranda. It was a beautiful, clear Montana late spring morning. She breathed deeply of the clean air and sipped her coffee as she watched Gary in the nearby practice ring, schooling a horse. Her Jeep, dew drenched, seemed to stare accusingly and remind her of an unfinished chore. Next to the kitchen door, attached to the house, there was a tool shed, unlocked. She swung open the creaking door and stared into the murky interior. When her eyes adjusted, she saw rows of neatly stowed yard tools. On a shelf, she discovered a 12-volt battery, coiled about it a jumper cable.

She set her coffee cup down, tested the battery, got a healthy spark, and then lugged it and the cable to her Jeep.

Gary, busy at the barn, heard a car start. He looked up to see that Kelly had gotten the Jeep running. He smiled in quiet amusement at her expertise at this, a man's work, and resumed his chores.

At the kitchen door, Gary's mother, back from her morning egg gathering, frowned as she noted Kelly's preparation to depart. She set down her eggs, picked up the piece of pipe suspended from the iron triangle meal summoner and vigorously activated it. Above the clamor she yelled, "Come and get it 'fore I throw it out." With a parting look in Kelly's direction, she disappeared into the kitchen.

The Jeep back in running order, Kelly promptly responded to her hostess's meal summons. She replaced the borrowed equipment and climbed the steps to the kitchen door. Before entering, her gaze was drawn back to Gary. She watched him release the colt to the freedom of the ring to celebrate with spirited airborne leaps and feisty kicks involving all fours. She watched Gary deftly coil the lunge line and hang it on its peg by the barn door. She liked the way he moved but as he now moved toward her Kelly suddenly became aware of the need to freshen up.

She ducked into the house and an amazingly short time later when she joined Gary at the breakfast table, Kelly wore a fresh shirt, her nails and face were scrubbed, and she smelled faintly of jasmine.

"I see you got your Jeep running," was Gary's opening line. He had started to rise and pull out a chair for her but Kelly quickly waved him off and seated herself.

He wore his hat at the table Kelly observed, which she would discover later was *de rigueur* for cowboys who seem to feel naked when bareheaded.

Marge Hunnicutt approached from the stove bearing two steaming platters of steak and eggs, three, and a heaping helping of home fried potatoes.

Kelly's Quest

"I hope you're hungry, child," Marge said as she set them down on the table. "Did you sleep well?"

"Like a stone," Kelly said, "and I'm ravenous."

There was butter, honey, and a plate of hot biscuits on the table, also steak sauce and ketchup, which Gary offered before he applied them generously to his food.

"You want cream for your coffee?" Marge asked.

"Yes please, if it's no trouble." Kelly replied.

"No trouble at all," Marge said as she went to the refrigerator.

"Where you headed from here?" Gary asked, as he chewed on a mouthful of steak.

Such an innocent question, yet it threw Kelly into mental turmoil. The truthful answer should have been "No place in particular." But that might have sounded like "fishing" for an invitation to stay on, which was, she suddenly realized exactly what she really wanted to do. She decided to be truthful. "I'm sort of exploring," she said. "I've never seen this part of the world."

"Well, there's a lot of it to see," Gary responded warmly. "I don't want to sound like the Chamber of Commerce, but if you like scenery, we've got it. If you like history, we've got that too. How about Custer's Last Stand? I tell you what's a fact, I saw a lot of country on the rodeo circuit, but I never yet saw a place I'd trade to live in."

Before he had finished speaking the phone rang. It was a wall phone next to the kitchen door. Marge answered it. "Hello, JB Ranch." Gary listened for a clue to the identity of the caller. His mother's cold next line, "Just a minute, I'll see if he's in," got him up.

She wordlessly handed him the receiver and joined Kelly at the table. She poured herself a cup of coffee and sat down.

Gary's phone conversation was low and confidential except for the chuckles. These, when they occurred, intensified the grimness of the set of Mrs. Hunnicutt's jaw.

Kelly felt the tension in the room and tried to alleviate it with conversation. "What a wonderful breakfast! I've never eaten steak and eggs for breakfast. This meal is going to take me down the road a piece. I won't have to stop for lunch."

To Kelly's surprise, her remarks got Marge's riveted attention. She fixed Kelly with a searching look, abruptly rose and said, "Excuse me," and disappeared out the kitchen door.

Alone at the table, Kelly prudently finished her breakfast.

When Gary finished his phone conversation he hung up, thought a beat, then started for the kitchen door when it occurred to him that he had a guest and an unfinished breakfast at the table. He stopped to apologize. "Sorry. Got to get a horse ready to show. Glad to have met you. Have a nice trip." With that, he was out the door.

She studied his half-eaten breakfast and hated the unknown phone caller who had control over this man. Kelly watched him go. She had no right to feel the way she did, but the delicious hint of wicked excitement she had felt the night before, when this attractive cowboy had lassoed her Jeep and was towing her to "his place," that was gone now. In its place was a sense of defeat.

Marge, she noted, was gone too. She might as well pack, she thought, and be on her way. Marge was not in the house so Kelly made up her bunk and wrote a thank-you note, which she left on her pillow. As she carried her bags to the Jeep, Kelly gave a last pensive look toward Gary over at the barn, schooling another horse.

She loaded her bags, slipped behind the wheel, reluctant to start the engine. When Kelly finally hit the starter button, she almost welcomed the empty dry rattle of an engine not starting.

That is when she became aware of Marge's appearance next to the Jeep. Wordlessly she handed Kelly a piece of wire and began to talk. "I don't beat around the bush child, I disabled your wheels."

Mechanically, Kelly took the connection and searched Marge's face for an explanation. Marge charged on.

"That boy needs a wife."

The double whammy of the disabled wheels and now this blunt approach to whatever was coming left Kelly with no options but to wait for Marge's next line.

"In my world, you judge stock and humans fast. I like you. Don't know what your situation is, but I'm not about to let you drive outta here without making a play. Now, he's still grieving over that Billie Jean Garner who threw him over to take up with that no-good Slade boy. You ask me, she did him a favor."

"You and I know a man don't know what's good for him. We've gotta maneuver him into it. So, I want to strike a deal with you. I know you can't force these things, so all I'm asking is, you stick around here a week and let's see what happens. If it's no dice, you're on your way. Let's say I asked you to stay on and help with the spring house cleaning. What'd'ya say? Is it a deal?"

Kelly's mind spun with an assimilation problem. Her modest mental computer raced, not unhappily, to sort out a prudent reply to this astounding input. To the image of Gary and the chance of another go at him, it was saying, *Yes! Yes! Yes!* On the downside, caution lights flashed. *Watch it, girl! Think it over! Look before you leap!* But there was no time to think it over.

"Well, Mrs. Hunnicutt," Kelly began. She narrowly avoided the cliché, 'This is so sudden.'

Then the answer flashed. *Yes.* But don't appear too eager. Shade it. Somewhere between *Yes* and *hard to get*.

"The name is Marge," Gary's mother reminded her.

"Well, Marge," Kelly corrected. "This would require a complete rescheduling of my travel plans – but–," she felt Marge's expectant stare. "You Hunnicutts are so charming, you make it difficult to say no."

"Good, then it's a deal," Marge said. And that was the way it was settled.

Gary accepted Kelly's presence on the ranch with polite indifference, apparently preoccupied with chores.

Kelly's own chore assignment was not heavy, but Marge's spring house cleaning was thorough. What needed to be scrubbed, dusted, aired, vacuumed or polished was accomplished as the two women worked side-by-side, conversing, trading life experiences, and gaining respect for each other.

Kelly earned added points by rewiring a prized lamp that had never worked. Outside, she gathered eggs laid by hens wily enough to survive the raids of marauding foxes.

Kelly's Quest

Since she was a horticulturist, Kelly took a special interest in cultivating the vegetable garden and attacking bugs in the potato patch.

One day while Marge had taken the truck to Showlo for groceries, and Gary was in the ring schooling a horse, the phone rang. Since Kelly was in the kitchen washing the breakfast dishes, the phone at her elbow, she dried her hands and picked up the receiver.

"Hello. JB Ranch."

A young female voice with a pronounced Texas accent answered. "Hah y'all, this is . . ." She half swallowed the name "Billie Jean," and challenged, "Wait a minute. Who are you?"

"I'm Kelly. What can I do for you?"

"I want to talk to Gary." It was a command.

"He is presently unavailable. Would you care to leave a message?"

Aware of whom she was addressing and with full knowledge of the background, Kelly was enjoying the encounter.

"Just tell Gary, Billie Jean called. No, wait." There was a change of tone that came on like an edict.

"Tell Gary I've decided to ride Dancer in the barrel race Saturday. Tell him to have the horse at Slade's show ring by ten o'clock."

It was a command.

"Is that all?"

"No. Tell him to call me."

"And your name is?" There was steam in Billie Jean's response.

"Billie Jean Garner."

"Does he know your number?"

"As well as he knows his name, honey."

On this parting shot, Billie Jean hung up.

When Gary came in for a drink of cold water, Kelly gave him the message. He took it without comment and picked up the phone.

Kelly pointedly afforded him privacy by finding a reason to retire to her room.

Later when Gary returned to the barn and Marge returned from town, Kelly related the happening as they stowed the groceries.

"Aggressive little bitch," Marge commented. "Gary should never have started lending her that horse. If Dancer comes up lame, he's a candidate for Calcan. Shit!"

Marge slammed down a can of beans on the kitchen table and took a contemplative pause. "Well, we've got to put our heads together and come up with something." They resumed stowing groceries until Marge stopped and snapped her fingers. "I've got an idea." Kelly stopped and listened.

Marge continued, "We'll lend her the horse, but you go with it."

"Me?" Kelly questioned.

"And Gary of course."

"What will that get us?" Kelly asked.

"Maybe nothing," Marge acknowledged. "You never know. But you there with Gary, puts the ball in her court."

And so a ploy was hatched: a Saturday night trip to town as a reward for Kelly's help around the house. But there was a hitch—Gary.

Kelly's Quest

He had already arranged for Slade's boy, Tonto, to pickup Dancer and haul him to Slade's. He, Gary, was going to be busy rounding up and shipping calves between now and Saturday and wasn't sure he wanted to attend the event anyway, at least Kelly assumed, not with her.

On Wednesday, the big truck, packed with calves destined for the railroad loading dock to weigh in for shipping, would not start.

Gary worked frantically on the stubborn engine, while the truckload of bawling critters steadily lost weight through natural elimination processes, at 23 cents a pound.

Frustrated, he disappeared into the house to make a phone call. When he returned, Kelly had the truck running.

She met his open-mouthed amazement with the magician's cool, never revealing for a second her lesson about condensation in the distributor, which had been taught to her by Duke a long time ago.

As for Gary, his wonder was such that turning the truck around, he backed into a tree. The profitable calf weigh-in at the loading dock seemed to provide a salutary effect on Gary's mood. He was suddenly amenable to Marge's plan.

A convivial Saturday night on the town was just the relaxation Kelly and Gary needed and now looked forward to. She bathed and dressed early to clear the bathroom for him and chose to wear, instead of her usual jeans, a period western dress adorned with cute buttons and bows. She had bought it years before to go Western dancing at the Crazy Horse Saloon.

When Gary, scrubbed, combed, and arrayed in his go-to-town best, made his appearance, Kelly felt a warm glowing pride at being his date. He was the "Marlboro Man" she had first glimpsed when her Jeep had stalled, but with slicked up improvements. The hat was new, a straw Resistol with a shape that reeked of authenticity. The pink western shirt was also new.

A cowboy in pink? Pink on Gary did not seem at all out of place. She particularly liked the way he smelled. It was a sort of leather, tobacco, and freshly laundered "man" smell that kindled in her a strange excitement. What touched her most was Gary's little-boy appeal when he presented her with a corsage of handpicked wild flowers, as they boarded his new pick up.

On the ride into Showlo both Gary and Kelly now looked at each other through new eyes, warily. They kept the conversation impersonal. They talked about cutting horses.

As they approached the turnoff leading into Slade's Casino parking lot, traffic slowed to a crawl. Vehicles were directed into the lot by a uniformed armed guard. Taking advantage of the congestion, a man, an Indian obviously from his features and garb, limped from vehicle to vehicle passing out flyers.

Since he walked with a cane, he took the flyers from a bag around his neck. When he arrived at Gary's truck, Gary greeted him familiarly. "How's it going, Richard?"

"I'm still here," the Indian said unsmiling as he handed Gary two flyers and moved along.

Gary glanced at the flyers, then laid them on the seat next to him.

Kelly, transfixed by the Indian's piercing black eyes, turned to follow his progress toward the next vehicle. "Who was that?" she asked.

"Richard Lightfoot," Gary said. "A local character."

Kelly's Quest

Kelly perused a flyer. She read aloud the bold print, "Slade's Stateline Casino. Unfair to Indians."

At her questioning look, Gary said, "It's a long story." He squeezed his way successfully into a vacant parking space. As they approached the arena behind the casino, decorated with balloons and gaily-colored pennants flapping in the breeze, Kelly's blood began to tingle with nervous anticipation.

The fruition of her accepted mission, to defuse this sex bomb, Billie Jean, and somehow immunize Gary Hunnicutt to her virus, began to assume unanticipated dimensions. In essence, that was the fanciful deal she had made with Marge. But, her first look at Billie Jean in action gave her pause.

Astride Gary's borrowed stud Dancer, she brilliantly performed feats of calf penning, independent of her supporting two-man team members, which brought cheers from the crowd in the bleachers. Then for an encore, she won the barrel-racing event. As if Billie Jean's sterling performance was not enough, a sidelong glance at Gary's beatific look crash-tested Kelly's morale. During the ribbon presentations, Kelly caught the too-casual exchange between them.

The look Billie Jean reserved for Kelly was disquieting. Billie Jean was not a local girl. Like a stray comet she blew into town from the great open spaces of Texas as the flashy focal point of a traveling western group, "The Waco Wackos." They were booked into Slade's State Line Corral for a week.

When they left, Billie Jean stayed as Jack Slade's girl of the moment until she saw Gary Hunnicutt, with whom she enjoyed a brief fling until Slade won her back with the gift of the red Mercedes convertible she drove. That was about the time the gambling deal went through with the Showlo Indian Tribe and suddenly Slade was rich.

Billie Jean was not unattractive. She had a traffic-stopping body, usually encased in weathered, skin-tight jeans, and ornate western shirts, form-fitted, but allowing for slight titillating movement of her unfettered breasts.

Her boots were expensive Lucace custom jobs, alligator, silver trimmed. Her championship silver belt buckle was man-sized and ornate, legitimately acquired. She had won it barrel racing at an Abilene Rodeo when she was sixteen. Her hat was a straw Resistole. Looking out from under its brim were two green eyes, a heart-shaped face crowned with naturally wavy auburn hair. A stab of red marked her mouth.

The words that came from it in a Texas tongue were brassy and bold, especially when she sang her number-one request, something about a silver dollar going from hand to hand, just as a woman goes from man to man.

In the ways of the world, using ancient stratagems, Billie Jean Garner had staked out a domain.

Geographically, it encompassed Slade's State Line Corral, adjoining lands, and certain subjects residing therein, including Slade himself, and through him, power over his minions.

This was Billie Jean's turf, space where Billie Jean ruled and no subject, particularly a special one named Gary Hunnicutt, was going to sashay into this place accompanied by an interloper, especially a pretty one.

Slade's was jammed and jumping. "The Sons of the Cousins of the Pioneers" Western band responded to the lift of a raucous Saturday night crowd.

Kelly's Quest

After dancing the "Texas Two-Step" enough to develop a thirst, Gary and Kelly were seated at a table, enjoying drinks.

Billie Jean, having finished her ever-popular rendition of the song about a woman, like a silver dollar, going from man to man, proceeded to demonstrate it.

Slade, in the cashier's cage, watched as she crossed the dance floor to Gary and flopped herself down on his lap. She addressed him in a Texas accent almost parodic in flavor.

"Wheah ya'll bin keeping yo'self, strangah?" she drawled. "Ah figgered y'all mus be dayed or somthin' leaving me all alone lahk thaut, you mallo hombre, you. Por que?" She tugged possessively on his braided leather string tie.

Gary grinned. *"Becerro tiempo el ranchero."*

Billie Jean's lip curled. *"Si, Señor,* calving time. Tell me about it." She stared at Kelly.

Gary made the introduction, which Kelly acknowledged with a nod and a stiff smile.

Billie Jean with a, "Hah y'all", a beat of cool stare. Then her eyes quickly shot back to Gary.

He tried to rise. "Let me get you a chair."

Billie Jean stopped him. "Why? Ah lak it heah." She gave her cute butt a tiny wiggle and stayed put. She took off his hat and put it on her head.

Hackles rising, Kelly made one obligatory try at civility, while the cogs of her mind whirled in search of a commanding handle to this situation. "Congratulations on winning the barrel race this afternoon."

Billie Jean sniffed. "Oh thaut? Thanks fo' nuthin' - no competition."

Gary offered, "Billie Jean won the southwestern barrel racing championship in Waco when she was sixteen."

"Wrong! Abilene," Billie Jean corrected. She rose and thrust her pelvis toward Gary's face for him to read the lettering on her belt buckle.

Gary shrugged. "Sorry, Abilene."

Resuming her position on his lap, Billie Jean studied Kelly a beat before she beamed a broad friendly smile. "Ah love yore drayus, buttons an' bows. Ah used to weah those thangs yeahs ago. Kind of a shitty color, but it's so you. You know what ah mean?"

Kelly put a wicked spin on her reply. "Yeah, honey, Ah know jes wha ch'all mean."

Billie Jean shot her a cold stare, then snuggled up closer to Gary, giving him a fat kiss on the mouth.

At this point, somehow Kelly's drink got upset, totally spilling into Billie Jean's lap.

She jumped up and frantically brushed off the wetness, lasering murder at Kelly. Billie Jean's raucous, "Goddamn, you did that a purpose," got room-wide attention. She picked up Gary's beer, and let Kelly have it full in the face.

A spectator screamed.

There was a beat of inaction, while Kelly wiped the beer from her eyes. Then, coolly shifting gears, from ladylike behavior to the level of what she encountered, Kelly rose to the challenge and the battle was joined.

Billie Jean was strictly a scratch, bite, and hair puller, while Kelly, fighting off Billie's clinch, sought an opening for her basic weapon, a hard right to the jaw.

The spectators, recovering from their initial shock, picked sides and boisterously shouted encouragement.

Slade, who had watched from the cashier's cage as the encounter developed, now moved in. He crossed the dance floor and grabbed Kelly.

Gary grabbed Billie Jean, separating the combatants.

Security took control of the still-belligerent Billie Jean while Slade, enjoying the contact, reluctantly turned over control of Kelly to Gary. They were near the exit to the parking lot when Slade said it.

"Say Gary, my girl still seems to have the hots for you, and your girl turns me on. Why don't we switch?"

His nasty smirk as he said it made the remark an unignorable insult.

Already adrenaline charged, Kelly's hair triggered, response was an automatically cocked fist and the classic Western barroom battle cue. "Why you—!"

Gary, with a negative shake of his head, deftly restrained her. Then without loss of motion, he pivoted, and swinging from the floor, caught Slade on the chin with a haymaker.

Slade hit the floor sliding.

The barroom crowd went wild.

Buddy Ebsen

Chapter Nine

Clothes are important, Kelly recalled later. If she had worn jeans instead of a dress that night, what happened later might not have happened.

From a peak of excitement, on a euphoric parachute floating down to a happy valley, in emotional territory new to her, Kelly silently watched Gary drive slowly toward home through the balmy skin-caressing moonlit night. "Her man" had fought for her. It didn't occur to her till later that she also had fought for him. She studied his handsome, sun-bronzed face, his slim, hard-muscled body, the sly grin as he stole occasional glances from the road.

Kelly couldn't remember at what particular instant it triggered her action; she only remembered an overpowering desire to kiss this man's mouth. So she did. Not just once. She swarmed over him so that he prudently pulled off the road.

Kelly drew away. Her own uninhibited boldness did not shock, but did surprise her. Was it too much? "Is anything wrong?" she asked.

Gary grinned. "Not in my book."

The beckoning chemistry of him created more desires. Because she very much wanted to, she boldly opened his shirt to better feel the naked, hard muscles of his body, the exciting feel of the hair on his chest.

With his left hand, unhurried, deliberate, Gary turned off the ignition. Then he took charge.

His kisses initially, Kelly noted, were rather firm and unschooled, but her mouth softened them. Then she felt his hands exploring, shyly at first.

Later, as she reviewed events, she decided she had made the right choice—wearing the dress.

The action that followed was almost wordless. Total mutual understanding of objectives and resultant cooperation removed the necessity for talk.

To those who hold it can't properly be done in the cab of a pickup, Kelly would argue that for the awkwardness, there are compensations, a sweet, heady craziness, and the devilish excitement of stealing apples.

At breakfast, Kelly and Gary's new looks at each other, their touchings, and Gary's obvious stumbling attentions to Kelly's every need were all "Ma" Hunnicutt required to convey that her plot was working, that last night "it" must have happened, a cause for rejoicing, despite the unanticipated twinge every mother must feel at the impending "loss" of her son to another woman.

Later that day, she made a pleasing discovery. The corrosive nagging pain in her gut had gone away. However, evaluating the inevitable waves made by the fight, red lights flashed on in her head. "Slade is not a forgiver," she warned. The wound of public humiliation on his own turf would fester. With Billie Jean to pick at the scab, it spelled bad days ahead for Hunnicutts and friends.

Gary shrugged. "He asked for it. What did you want me to do?"

"Just what you did son," Marge replied. "Long as you keep in mind, you haven't heard the last of this."

Kelly recalled the way the fight started and felt guilty. "It was my fault," she blurted out. "I spilled the drink on Billie Jean, but I didn't expect it would start a feud."

"Start a feud?" Marge snorted.

Gary grinned.

"That happened a hundred years ago."

"At least," Gary agreed.

At Kelly's questioning look, Marge continued.

"The original Jack Slade was—"

"Named Jake," Gary corrected.

With a leveling look at her son, Marge continued. "Alright, Jake."

"Jake Slade was hanged by vigilantes from the balcony rail of his hotel in 1860, and there was a Hunnicutt in the mob that did it."

"Hanged?" Kelly's eyes widened.

"By the neck until dead," Marge continued. "Because his hotel was a notorious robber's roost. It stood exactly where the state line gambling joint stands today."

"Or so they say," Gary amended.

"Why did they hang him?" Kelly wanted to know.

"He was a road agent," Gary replied. At Kelly's questioning look, he continued, "A highway holdup man, a robber."

"Today," Marge chimed in, "his great, great, great grandson, Jack Slade, on the same location, is doing the same thing with mechanical 'one armed bandits.'"

Kelly had another question.

"When we were at Slade's yesterday, I was introduced to that funny little man, Chief Shaggy Bear. Is he really chief of the Showlo Indian Tribe?"

Gary nodded. "Far as I know."

"Then don't the Indians own the casino?"

Gary and his mother exchanged a look.

"That question," Gary replied, "is what lawyers like to refer to as moot."

Marge rose, smiling. "How about a recess counselor, while I brew us some fresh coffee?" She headed for the stove.

Gary used this moment of privacy to lift Kelly's hand and kiss it. Though they exchanged quiet possessive smiles, Kelly's heart beat wildly, remembering the intimacies of the previous night.

When Gary lit a cigarette, he offered one to Kelly, who declined while making a protective mental note to prevail on this suddenly special guy to duck the habit.

"To answer your question, don't the Indians own the casino?" Gary began. He took a thoughtful drag and exhaled before answering, "They don't. The property on which the casino stands, along with a big hunk of surrounding range was owned by Slade. The story, for what it's worth, of how he acquired it is that one of his great-great grandfathers won it with a "Showlo" poker hand. Slade's partner, George Mayfield, is president of the Showlo Bank and Trust Company. It's a small bank, but with 'connections,' if you know what I mean."

"You asked me about that Indian passing out flyers yesterday. That was Richard Lightfoot. He is the grandson of Chief Shaggy Bear, the present chief, and is campaigning to take his place. The Showlo Indians are a splinter tribe of Sioux or Chippewa, I think. For years they's been pestering Indian Affairs for tribal recognition and a hunk of government land for a reservation."

"Mayfield saw this as the makings of a deal. So he flew to Washington. If there is one thing George Mayfield knows, it's his way around alleys to back doors in Washington and how to collect on campaign contributions."

"Using his political savvy plus 'smoke and mirrors,' he came home with the bacon. By having Slade deed the Indians enough land to qualify as a bona fide tribe, he maneuvered their case through the National Indian Gaming Commission, got them a gaming license, and they were in business."

"The Indians?"

Gary took a drag, exhaled, and shook his head. "No, Slade and Mayfield. The Indians, as usual, got the dirty end of the stick, or the crumbs that fell from Slade and Mayfield's table."

In retrospect, Kelly knew that the big winner after the battle at Slade's place, not even present that night, had been Marge Hunnicutt.

Her ploy had paid off. Billie Jean was out.

Kelly also felt victorious, but celebrated cautiously. The events of the past several weeks now occasioned a look-back moment, a study of her wake since she departed home to take off on a new course.

She fought periodic moments of guilt when Pop's charge haunted her, *You're a loose canon Kelly, slamming around, knocking people's lives out of kilter.* She struggled to justify her past conduct. She did feel some responsibility in that her actions had jeopardized the livelihood of her brothers and that she had run away without leaving so much as a forwarding address. That had prompted her to send a postcard to Kevin. But in weighing the merits and demerits of Kelly Ryan's personal balance sheet, one shining positive outweighed all negative items.

Gary Hunnicutt!

If ever a girl was instinctively searching for a Mr. Right, and she was, every cell in her body, every particle of her being shrieked that she had found him. The question now cudgeling Kelly's mind was, 'How do I make him mine, totally and forever?' Having witnessed Gary's obvious high regard for Billie Jean's horsemanship, Kelly realized in that area, she was vulnerable.

In order to win permanently this chosen man, she reasoned, she must weave around his heart those invisible silken threads that would make him now and forever hers, even if it meant becoming a champion barrel racer.

Chapter Ten

"Now here's what you've got to remember, Kelly." Gary told her several days later as he snapped the left stirrup leather taut and cinched up the saddle. Maintaining light hand contact with the horse's rump, he moved around it to shorten the other stirrup.

Kelly, seated in the saddle, paid strict attention. Ever since she witnessed Billie Jean "shine" in the barrel racing, Kelly, a born competitor, had maintained a subtle siege on Gary to teach her that skill.

It had bugged her to learn that the horse Billie Jean rode that day had been borrowed for the occasion from Gary's string. It was in fact, Dancer, the mount on which Kelly was presently seated, and that Gary had immediately reclaimed after the ruckus at Slade's.

"They say horses are dumb," Gary began, "but this horse knows more about you from the moment you get aboard than you know about him. He's called a cutting or reining horse because of the way he is trained to respond to the handling of the reins. If you want him to go to the left you lay the rein on the right side of his neck. To go to the right you do just the opposite. If you want him to go forward you don't have to spur or whip or kick him, you just squeeze with your knees with a slack rein. If you want him to back up you tug evenly and gently on both reins." He paused. "Have you got that?"

Kelly nodded confidently. "I read all that in the book," she said impatiently.

"Alright, smarty," Gary responded. "Now remember this. If you are cutting out or penning a calf, to a good mount, it's a game. And Dancer is a good mount, aren't you boy?" Gary gave the horse a couple of cupped hand claps on the withers, to which Dancer responded with a mane shake and a snort. "Entering into the game, sometimes he will react instinctively to the calf's moves. He may make a ninety-degree change of direction from south to east at top speed, without command. Unless you are ready for that, you will continue to go south airborne and wake up smelling clover. Any questions?"

Kelly, grinning at his pedantry, shook her head.

"Alright, we'll start with a simple exercise. See the barrels over there?"

Gary indicated a nearby line of white barrels spaced ten yards apart. To Kelly's confident "Yep," he ordered, "Walk the horse through them Slalom style."

It was easy. She did it perfectly.

"Good," Gary commented as she finished. "Now do it again." She did it three times.

The fourth time, Dancer, apparently bored with this pony-ride, kid stuff, broke into an easy lope.

Kelly, her body not yet schooled to that accommodating pelvic movement that keeps the seat in the saddle while the torso undulates, was standing in the stirrups, bumping, completely out of sync.

Dancer, knowing the course, took charge at his own pace, which was fast.

Kelly hung on past three barrels and panicked. Yanking on the reins, she gave Dancer mixed signals. He made a right angle turn; Kelly was airborne and woke up smelling clover.

In true cowboy priority, Gary secured the loose horse first. A thrown rider is not a five-alarm catastrophe in Montana, but since it was Kelly, he moved as fast as Dancer, under tow, would allow.

Kelly was uninjured, embarrassed, and giggling as he helped her to rise.

"Anything hurt?"

Kelly groaned. "Just my pride."

"That was a pretty bad fall. You'll feel it tomorrow."

They started to walk back toward the barn.

Kelly stopped. "Aren't I supposed to get right back on and ride again? Isn't that what they say?"

"What who say?"

"I don't know. I read it in the book."

Gary grinned. "You can if you want to, personally I don't recommend it. You worried me enough for today."

Kelly gave him a big, warm smile and touched his hand at this shy expression of concern. Since the intimacy they had shared in the truck, Gary's manner toward her had been impeccable. While thoughts of that night occupied his mind with endless enthrallment, there was no loutish, taken-for-granted familiarity, just a gentleman's respect for a lady's mood that might be transient.

Kelly found this shyness becoming, in fact alluring. She had wild thoughts about another trip to town in the truck.

The distinctive throb of a helicopter swiveled their heads. As it came in, flying directly over the house, somebody aboard waved.

Gary returned the wave. "That's Charlie Sheldon. Wonder what he wants?" The chopper banked sharply, and gently eased down in the center of the parking area.

When the blades stopped rotating, there was a beat before a door popped open and a man's figure emerged. It was Noel DeLacey.

Kelly's stunned reaction was a questioning yell. "Noel?" Noel responded with a delighted shout, "Kelly!" and he bounded to her for the "clinch."

Chapter Eleven

Kelly gushed delightedly. "Noel! - How in the world?"

He cut in. "It's a long story."

As the chopper pilot joined them, there were introductions followed by an awkward moment of conversational stall. To relieve it, Gary tactfully broke off to lead the horse to the barn; Charlie Sheldon tagged along.

Gary hitched Dancer to the hot walker and began to remove the saddle. Noel and Kelly, deep in animated conversation, strolled. Their bursts of laughter drifted back, claiming Gary's scowling attention.

Sheldon made no comment.

It was Gary who broached the subject. As he slid the saddle off Dancer's back, he jerked his head in the direction of the strolling pair. "Who is this guy?"

Charlie shrugged. "I was just about to ask you the same question."

Standing at the kitchen door, dishcloth in hand, Marge Hunnicutt, who had watched the scene, also pondered it.

Kelly, who had "belonged" to nobody upon her arrival at the ranch, was to discover she now apparently, by just being herself, had won a place in the lives of three people.

Noel and Kelly talked for an hour. They sat for a while on the bench in the shade of the big cottonwood talking, seemingly unconscious of the passage of time.

It surprised Kelly that she still harbored some curiosity about the Hollywood scene, news of which Noel poured out with enthusiastic embellishment. Then his manner changed and Kelly surmised she was about to hear his message.

"I don't know how to begin to say this, Kelly, this and all the things I am about to tell you. So, I'll start from my beginnings," was Noel's portending preamble.

"I was born sensitive, with latent artistic perceptions that enabled me to feel more than what I had knowledge of. My father never understood me, but my mother did. All beauty stems from harmony, which I believe is the Divine intent. I strongly felt the compulsion to bring harmony to troubled people by using the talents God gave me. That is why I created this simple human story, *Joey*.

"The truth, Kelly, is that *Joey*, in spite of its virtues, might never have seen the light of day, except for what I perceive to be Divine intervention. And that was you. It was no accident that we met, Kelly. It was part of a master design of which everything is now falling into place, as it was meant to. The nuts and bolts of it is that Manny Gold, head of GTR, the most powerful talent agency in the world, believed in me so much, he has convinced Midas, a European money source, to finance whatever I want to do next."

His eyes locked with Kelly's. "Do you know what that means? In this gross, money-grubbing business, Kelly, this is a miracle! And you supplied the key to it, the key to my future. You are my good-luck charm, my rabbit's foot, my security blanket, if you will. You supplied the validation to my belief in myself. I can't afford to lose you, Kelly."

He stopped talking and stared at her. "Now, here comes the sixty-four-dollar question. Will you come back with me and help bring about the wondrous happenings that even now are bubbling from my creative soul. I need you. Will you? Will you, Kelly? Please."

The unexpected switch from soaring eloquence to little-boy appeal made Kelly laugh. "You're funny," was her response.

Noel frowned. "That's no answer. How am I funny?"

Kelly responded. "Well, look at the situation. I midnight requisitioned you a little equipment and climbed a utility pole to get you some 'juice.' Does that qualify me to be an assistant moviemaker? Of course not. You're off and running now. God bless. Enjoy. You don't need me. You just think you do."

Noel seized the opening. "And that is precisely my point, Kelly. I am not so naïve as to believe there will be no rough days ahead. There will be lots of them. That is when I will need you to stand by my side and sustain my confidence. Kelly, we can conquer the world together."

Kelly fielded a puzzling flash. Was this a proposal or just a proposition?

Back in the ranch house kitchen, over the second steaming pot of Marge's brew, the Hunnicutts exchanged small talk after they had exhausted discussion of what Charlie had to say about his mysterious passenger. The 10:32 from Salt Lake City had deposited this "live one" at the Billings airport that morning. He had walked into Charlie's place of business and booked a ride to a location Charlie knew as well as he knew his own address.

For Charlie, the thousand-dollar, round-trip tab was "found money" with a bonus, a chance to visit old friends. He would have done it for the gasoline money. While Gary, dark-faced, looked out the window, Charlie looked at his watch and announced, "We should be starting back soon. It's a three hour flight, and I prefer to do it by daylight."

His concerns were voided when Kelly and Noel made a buoyant entrance to encounter questioning stares.

Introductions made and hospitality stiffly proffered, Noel, sensing immediately the cool formality of the meeting, became aware of the time. He hurriedly said his goodbyes and led the group toward the chopper, talking with Kelly each step of the way. Apologizing profusely for his unannounced intrusion, conversing as they went, he led the group toward the chopper. Before he unnecessarily but instinctively pulled in his neck to avoid the spinning blades, Noel embraced Kelly.

Above the idling chopper noise, Gary heard Noel's voice. "Think it over, Kelly, and let me know."

Gary, reading the embrace intently, saw only a hug and gallant kissing of her hand, no kiss on the mouth, which allowed his spirits to rise somewhat. He watched the helicopter disappear in the distance while the knot in his gut eased.

Noel's story, as Kelly related it to Gary and his mother, later, now sounded like a fairy tale too good to be true. Midas, a foreign capital source, looking for motion picture investment, had shrewdly analyzed Noel's film and the promise displayed in *Joey*. Such things do happen, but only to strangers, Kelly acknowledged.

But Galactic Talent Representation, through a memorandum agreement with Midas, had secured for Noel, at his curious insistence, an immediate green light to pick a "production assistant," ergo his successful search for the missing Kelly. That was a little hard to swallow. Her brother Kevin had been a factor, Kelly discovered. Noel had gotten the ranch address from the postcard Kelly had sent.

"When are you leaving?" Gary's delivery was quiet, blunt, poker faced, shielding freshly realized vulnerability.

Kelly winced. The line had impacted like a blow. "Am I being kicked out?"

Gary answered quietly. "I think you know better than that."

Marge Hunnicutt felt the chill and took a discrete exit, listening from the kitchen. Kelly and Gary's budding relationship unseasoned by time and common experience had hit an uncharted rock. They hardly knew each other. In the several weeks since she had arrived, that relationship had traveled from polite indifference to intimacy.

Until the helicopter delivered Noel, they were sailing along on a billowy cloud in a budding romance, thriving on fresh memories and mutual anticipation. Where had that gone?

Kelly studied Gary's handsome face. It bore an expression she had not seen there before, a brooding blend of hurt and something else. Accusation? "It's gone isn't it?" Her simple statement was quiet, introspective, like a researcher's discovery of a scientific fact.

"What is?" Gary knew, but wanted to hear it.

"What we had."

"What did we have?"

"Promise. The promise of something wonderful."

He did not respond

"It was there," Kelly spaced her thought significantly, "before the helicopter arrived."

Their eyes met.

"I didn't send for the helicopter. Or that particular passenger," Kelly stated defensively.

Gary thought a beat before he said, "Tell me about him."

Kelly, in a shoot-the-works mode, feeling she had nothing to hide, impulsively told him her life story; how she got to be where she was. She told him about Duke, then about Noel's entrance into her life. How they met, what happened, what didn't happen, and why Noel now apparently considered her a sort of security blanket, a good luck charm portending future success.

Long before Kelly finished her story, Gary had formulated in his mind the question he would ask when she finally stopped talking.

When that happened Kelly looked at him with a wan smile. "Any more questions?"

"Yes," Gary said. "I love you. Will you marry me?"

The 'sugar rush' racing through Kelly's body, healing everything that hurt, brought a smile starting deep within her, as she spoke the heartfelt truism. "I thought you'd never ask."

It took an hour to sort out their true feelings.

Marge, the while, found things to do quietly in the kitchen. Then, eavesdropping, she grinned triumphantly and wished she had a bottle of champagne. She settled for a half bottle of bourbon so that when, many kisses later, the two, now-pledged lovers, hand-in-hand, made their starry-eyed entrance, she was ready for them.

There were hugs and congratulations amid toasts to lifetimes of happiness and more hugs and after three belts of bourbon, admonishments from Marge about the severity of Montana winters and the hardships to be endured by ranch wives as opposed to the *dolce-vita*-life of Hollywood.

To Gary, the sudden gush of bosom closeness between his mother and Kelly sniffed of collusion. Had there been a plot? He remembered skittish stallions he had approached shaking a can of oats in one hand while concealing the bridle behind him in the other. Then he 'got it.' *Here Comes the Bridle.* He hummed the wedding march and grinned the wry grin of one cowboy quite willingly caught in the tender trap.

It was after midnight when the call came. Marge answered.

It was for Kelly, who was in the bathroom applying liniment to her fall-bruised body, the 'outlying precincts' of which were now being heard from.

She picked up the receiver and spoke a tentative, "Hello?" Then in full recognition of the answering voice.

"Kevin?" There were few audio clues and long listening silences, making it difficult for Marge to monitor the conversation.

"When did it happen?"

Another long silence. "What hospital?" There followed a flurry of fragmentary bits of conversation concluding with a "Hang in there Kevin, I'll call you in the morning."

Kelly hung up. Then finally, she responded to Marge's questioning stare. "Pop's had a stroke."

Buddy Ebsen

Chapter Twelve

By the time Gary returned from checking a ruckus at the horse barn, Kelly had decided. No matter what their parting relationship, Pop was her father. Without him, she would never have been. She had to go.

"It will only be temporary," she insisted. "Then I'll be back," she promised Gary. But the grinning demons of her mind fed unease.

There was barely time to pack and sleep four hours. Then, in the rush to Missoula to catch the Billings flight that connected with one to L.A., there were so many things to say, the new situation to accommodate to new feelings, new importance and in the rush, no time to express them.

With Gary driving at emergency speeds and then running with Kelly and her bags, they made it. At the gate, Kelly clutched him fiercely and poured into Gary's ear what spilled from her heart. "Darling, darling man, I have looked all my life for you, and now I no more want to get on that airplane than I want to die. Tell me I don't have to go," she begged. "Tell me there's nothing I can do for Pop that it's alright for me not to go, please."

Gary frowned. "That's what I'd like to do, but it's something only you can decide, Kelly. If you don't go, it could haunt you the rest of your life."

"I'll write everyday," she promised. "And I'll be back soon."

He attempted a cheerful grin. "I'll be waiting."

Kelly gave him a lingering kiss, then looked deeply into his eyes. "I love you, Gary."

"And I love you, Kelly," he responded simply. "I'll be waiting, and while I'm waiting . . ." He took from his pocket a small vintage jewel box and extracted from its plush-lined interior a gold ring mounted with a large square cut diamond. "It was my mother's," he explained. "Would you wear it?"

The full implication of what he had said rendered Kelly speechless. "Oh, Gary," she gasped and fumbled for more words. Then, concerned, "Your mother's?"

"She suggested it," he said as he slipped it on Kelly's finger.

Kelly's response was a helpless series of "Oh, Garys" and a tearful collapse into his arms.

Later, her heart bursting with love, she waved to him from the window, not sure that he saw her as the plane taxied out to the runway. She waved again to his solitary figure as the plane on takeoff came by, full throttle. Gary would watch she knew, until it became a speck in the sky.

Chapter Thirteen

Kevin and Junior met her at the airport. The scared-little-boy look in their eyes hit Kelly with a load of guilt. So dependant on Pop for jobs and strength, his collapse had knocked the props out from under both of them. She felt contrite for having vanished without a trace except for that one piddling postcard.

On the way to the hospital, conversation was sparse. Obviously, they blamed her for their father's stroke. Maybe they were right. She wished that she could have lived that part of her life over again. Her brothers had jobs to go to and left her at the hospital door.

When Kelly entered Pop's room she was alone for an instant with her father. It was the first time since he had struck her. The change in his appearance was shocking.

In spite of his age, the father she knew had always been florid-faced, vigorous, and vital. To see him lying there pale, hollow-cheeked, and helpless, sprouting a tangle of tubes and wires, he looked like someone she had never known. Kelly's initial shock dissolved into compassion.

A nurse entered. Brisk, businesslike, with only a perfunctory smile, she checked the monitor displaying Pop's heartbeats, made some notes on a clip board, checked the fluid level of the intravenous feeder, and left.

Kelly moved quietly toward the head of the bed. She found a chair, sat in it, and studied her father's face. A flood of memories moistened her eyes. "My name is MacNamara, I'm the leader of the band."

The leader was laid low now. Who would lead when he was gone? Gone? Pop Ryan gone? No! He must not be gone! She, Kelly Ryan willed him to live. She clenched fists and willed it until her body shook.

In the days that followed, Pop's sons came at visiting hours, but Kelly would not leave his side. She slept in the room on a roll-away cot for three nights. Her father had not opened his eyes. A parade of nurses moved silently in and out of the room checking equipment, making marks on clipboards. Periodically, doctors interrupted her vigil as she sat at Pop's bedside holding his hand.

The fourth night, as Father Hennesy made his late routine call, Kevin slept in the overstuffed chair, Junior on a sofa in the reception lounge. The heartbeats on the monitor were faint.

Father Hennesy looked out the window at the passing traffic. Kelly sat, both hands now clasping one of Pop's. She watched his heartbeats in the scope, quietly praying he would open his eyes so she could make her peace with him before he— she couldn't even think it. Pop was not going to die! She prayed it—willed it.

Father Hennesy looked down at Kelly, head bowed in fervent prayer. He knelt at her side and gently touched her arm. "Relax, Kelly. Be at peace. Remember, 'let Thy will, not my will, be done.'"

"I am a force majeure," Kelly responded fiercely, desperately. "Pop's not going to die!"

Kelly's Quest

Father Hennesy studied her a moment, rose, and resumed his post at the window.

There was a slight quickening on the scope recording Pop's heartbeats. Kelly anxiously searched his face. With his eyes open, his speech blurred, he spoke a single word, "Kelly?"

Tearfully, Kelly smiled, nodded her head convulsively, and clutched his hand tighter. "Yes, it's me, Pop. It's me, Kelly." Pop's brow furrowed as he struggled to say the next words, enunciating the thought that had been haunting him, torturing him, eating at his soul - "I struck you."

Kelly's tears were pouring now as she frantically struggled to deny the truth of it. "No! No! Pop, you didn't—besides I deserved it—I was an impossible brat. I had it coming—it didn't hurt. Oh, Pop - Pop, I love you."

She collapsed into sobs.

Pop's lips stubbornly repeated the words — "I struck you - and," then with great effort, "God struck me." Kevin was awake now and Father Hennesy had moved closer. "I deserve to die." He closed his eyes.

Kelly clutched his hand tighter, intermittently kissing it as she fiercely willed the words. "No! No! - You are not going to die. You are going to live, Pop. We're going to have wonderful times together again. You and Kevin and Junior and me—the way we used to."

With closed eyes, Pop faintly uttered three words – "Forgive me, Kelly."

Impulsively, Kelly embraced him. "Oh yes, yes, Pop, I forgive you. Do you hear me? Pop. I forgive you. Oh Pop."

She collapsed kneeling at his bedside, hugging his body.

The scope registered increasingly long intervals between heartbeats. The intern and a nurse re-entered the room. They checked the monitor and Pop's vital signs. Kelly quietly sobbed as Father Hennesy began the last rites.

Junior entered and, with Kevin, went to Kelly. They raised her to her feet and joined in a three-way hug. The nurse and intern departed, affording the grieving family privacy.

As Kelly remembered it, so it was until the "miracle." That came with an abrupt shuddering movement of Pop's body. Then a prolonged rumbling from deep within, followed by a series of belching, explosive emissions of gas. Simultaneously, the reading on the monitor jumped, stopped, then resumed with a vigorous steady beat.

It was hard to tell who in the room was more shaken, Father Hennesy, Kelly's brothers, or Kelly, all transfixed by what they were witnessing.

As the monitor continued to report that Pop was alive, Kelly's mounting ecstatic wonder was invaded by a scary thought. Might she have stepped on God's toes a little with her blatant insistence that she was a force majeure, an act of God? What if God hadn't liked that? She quickly said a small prayer asking for forgiveness. However, subsequent events gave no hint God had taken offense.

Medical journals reported the "miracle." Pundits wrote opinions about it. A priest claimed it a heaven-sent reward to Pop for service to the church, and it inspired a segment on the TV show "Believe It or Not".

At six o'clock the following morning, Pop, wide awake, was sitting up, demanding food.

Chapter Fourteen

On the phone to Gary, Kelly poured out her pent-up elation. "My precious love. I have such wonderful news! Pop is alive! He is sitting up right now eating breakfast. Isn't that wonderful? They say it's a miracle. It wasn't a stroke at all. I don't think they know what it was, and I don't care. Pop is alive! And I am on a cloud. You were so right my darling man, to make me come back. I can't thank you enough. It was so right, my being here."

Kelly stopped for breath. There was a long silence. Kelly broke it. "Gary? Gary are you there? Can you hear me?"

When Gary spoke, his tone, in contrast to hers, was subdued. "I'm happy to hear about your father, Kelly. How are you?"

Kelly bubbled on, "Wonderful, just wonderful, now."

"How long will he stay in the hospital?"

"They say a week for observation," Kelly answered. "Then home. I'm checking out a seniors' service to get a therapist that works with recovering patients. It sounds good."

"How are you getting around without wheels?" Gary asked.

"Okay, of course I miss my Jeep."

"It's sitting here looking lonely," Gary said, "and so am I."

There was in his tone something that took Kelly off the euphoric cloud provided by her father's miraculous recovery. It was a distant rumble of foreboding.

During the days and nights of Pop's crisis, every concern, every prayer, was for him. But now, something struck her, a sneak punch from the blind side. Kelly felt the stab of both horns of a dilemma. Her mind churned apprehensively. When will she be free to go to Gary? How long will they be apart? Does absence really make the heart grow fonder? Or, as the small grinning demon behind her kept whispering in her ear, "Sure it does, for somebody else."

Chapter Fifteen

Pop's recovery came in spurts with relapses.

In his high periods, he was his vital, cantankerous self. During the lows, he became the pitiable invalid Kelly found when she arrived at the hospital. His condition swings diminished some of the elation Kelly had felt at his miraculous recovery.

The home-care nursing service she had engaged was satisfactory, but they needed to be paid. So did the stack of accumulated medical bills. As Kelly was to learn, Pop's union's medical coverage sounded great, and it was in theory, but when you read the fine print, you discovered they questioned every item and paid only a portion of each claim.

Junior and Kevin helped some, but, as Kelly knew, Junior was paying alimony and child support while Kevin's wife had not been well since the birth of their baby. So Kelly shouldered the load and accepted responsibility for paying all Pop's bills.

Pop contributed to her problems by continually inviting young Terrence O'Malley to visit him and sneak in beer. Pop's insensitive nudging Kelly toward accepting this virtual clone of himself as a suitor for her hand in marriage drove Kelly a little nuts, but what could she do about it?

Nothing. She was helpless and trapped in her dedication to her father's welfare.

At six o'clock one morning, the Ryan doorbell rang. Kelly, barely awake, slipped on a robe and stumbled toward the door. Halfway there, she saw through the curtained window the figure of a tall man wearing a Western hat. Her heart jumped. "Gary?" She let out a whoop, flung open the door, but it wasn't Gary. The tall cowboy looked her over and grinned. "I'm sorry, ma'am, I'm Willford. Right now I wish I was Gary."

To cover Kelly's embarrassment he continued. "I brought you something." He led her outside to a dusty truck parked at the curb. Attached to the truck was a dusty horse trailer, two switching horsetails hanging over the tailgate. Hooked to the trailer with a tow bar was her Jeep.

The sight hit Kelly where she lived and brought tears. "That dear, beloved, thoughtful man," she mused, as she slowly shook her head. She turned to the cowboy. "And you, mister?" She paused.

"Just Willford," he volunteered.

Kelly smiled. "Alright, Mister Just Willford, how about some breakfast?"

Willford was busy unhooking the Jeep. "Thank you, ma'am, but I've got to get on down the road."

As Kelly helped roll her vehicle to the curb, she persisted. "I am so indebted to you. Can't I at least make you a cup of coffee?"

"Thanks a heap, ma'am," Willford replied, "but I've got to keep rolling. It's a fur piece to Abeline." He opened the door of his truck and turned to Kelly. "Gary was right about something." He climbed in and slammed the door.

"About what?" Kelly asked.

Willford stepped on the starter, the engine roared. He leaned out "You're the purtiest thing that ever come down the pike." He grinned, stepped on the gas pedal, and was gone.

Kelly watched him go. She smiled and felt a heart-warming glow.

Buddy Ebsen

Chapter Sixteen

It was a smoggy Los Angeles summer day. What air stirred came from a dying Santa Ana and put people in surly, sweaty moods.

The Roto Rooter truck parked curbside gave flagrant notice there was trouble at the Ryan residence. "Kids," the loquacious Rooter man snorted as he cranked the jumbo plumbers "snake" twenty feet into the Ryan plumbing. "How're you gonna teach kids a toilet is not a waste basket?"

"My father is no kid," Kelly said.

"Oh, second childhood huh?" the man quipped.

Kelly did not respond.

Pop was out. Junior, not working, had volunteered to take him for the day, first to the dentist, then to a Dodger game. Of the two therapists Kelly had arranged to handle such needs, Pop had fired one. The other had quit.

As Kelly wrote the check to pay off the plumber, she was made aware of something. Her bank balance was low. She tabled that problem for the moment and moved on to the next item on her "do" list: vacuum cleaning. The house shrieked for it. After the rugs came the curtains, which on touch launched clouds of accumulated dust that had not been disturbed since her mother died. It was hot work.

The phone rang. Kelly rather welcomed it. It gave her an excuse to sit down, wipe her dripping brow, and take a breather.

When she picked up the receiver, a familiar voice pounced on her "Hello?"

It was Noel. "Kelly!" The enthusiasm in his tone was engaging. "However are you? You have no idea of how much I have missed you, and how much I want to see you."

"That's nice," Kelly said. "And how are things with you?"

"Terrific!" Noel responded. "Absolutely beyond belief! I have so much to tell you. When can we talk? How about today?"

"Today?" Kelly was startled.

"How about fourish, we'll do tea in, get this, my new condominium. Wait till you see it, and I want you to meet someone."

"Who?" Kelly asked.

"Never mind, it's a surprise. Will you come?"

Taken aback, Kelly negated his pitch with a slow frustrated shake of her head. "Noel," she began. "It is sweet of you, but out of the question today. I am house cleaning. And there's my father. He's been very sick, you know, and he is now my responsibility."

"Kelly! I didn't know. Is there anything I can do?" He sounded sincere.

"Yes," Kelly replied. "Turn off the heat. I'm sweltering."

Noel pounced on this. "My condo is so cool. Even as I speak, I am wearing a jacket. Please, Kelly, won't you come?"

Kelly laughed at his persistence. "Your offer is very tempting."

"Please come before the heat gets you," Noel said. "Give me a call." He left a number.

As the pitiful breeze died, the humidity climbed, and the sweat poured. The urgency of house cleaning seemed more and more remote.

Kelly reviewed the last three weeks. She mentally churned the facts. Without relief, she had spent the time totally caring for her father. If anyone was entitled to a breather, a change of scene for a few hours, she was.

Actually, she could do a better job for Pop if she took a brief respite, she convinced herself, and called Noel. He was delighted. Armed with his address in West Hollywood, near the region of antiques, boutiques, and interior decorators, Kelly began to make plans. A shower and shampoo, of course, but what to wear?

Except for the buttons-and-bows dress she had worn "that night" and a few plain cotton numbers, her wardrobe might have been mistaken for her brothers.

However, she had once bought, on a whim against the day she might want to dress up like a lady, a flowered chiffon ensemble she had seen on a mannequin. It consisted of a wide, drooping, black straw-hat, black pumps, and black stockings to form a sort of protective parameter for the flowing softness of the dress. She found it in a basement storage closet. She also found a pair of black mesh gloves, tried them on, decided she would perhaps wear one and carry the other.

A full dress rehearsal with the small gold cross on a fine gold chain around her neck, and Gary's mother's engagement ring on her finger, allowed Kelly to ask her mirror: did she now personify the commercial, 'She's young, she's beautiful, she's engaged.' Kelly studied her reflection. Young and engaged perhaps, but beautiful? She wrinkled her nose in doubt.

But she was confident. No matter what surprise quest she was to encounter, she would be armored.

Chapter Seventeen

Noel DeLacey's mother was a genteel, soft-spoken Southern lady, but in her voice and about her refined manner, there were the faint receding echoes of the *Rebel Yell*, the *Bonnie Blue Flag* and *Dixie*.

Noel, in his newfound affluence, had brought her to California to savor his success.

She was a wisp of a lady with patrician features, a straight back, and clear steady eye. Her opening line after the introduction was, "And so you are Kelly," as she took in Kelly's rather smashing image, from stem to stern.

"Yes, I am," Kelly replied with a generous smile, inspired by the full knowledge that she was making an impression.

"I have heard and read nothing but Kelly, Kelly, Kelly, from Noel in the last month, and I must say, son, you did not exaggerate. She is charming."

Kelly beamed, and it flashed through her mind, 'nice things happened to you when you wore dresses.' She should wear them more often.

The meeting had begun well, Noel glowing as he conducted the tour of his extensive premises. When the phone rang, he delegated his mother to carry on the inspection tour while he picked up the receiver.

They had proceeded past a view of the Jacuzzi and into linen closets when Noel, crestfallen, caught up with them. "Wouldn't you know," he began. "My beloved agent just now informed me that I am an hour late for a meeting with some of the Midas top brass at the Polo Lounge. "Please have tea and stay on," he pleaded. "I will positively tear myself away as quickly as I decently can. Then we'll do dinner together." He gave his mother a hug, Kelly's hands a squeeze, and was off.

"My tea service was made in England," Mrs. DeLacey volunteered as she poured from a highly adequate porcelain teapot into Kelly's cup. "Do you prefer lemon or milk?"

They were seated at a Louis XIV tea table in the living room.

"Lemon, please," Kelly said.

As she passed the lemon, Noel's mother continued to describe her tea set, "The silversmith was Paul Revere's great grandfather."

"Oh," Kelly said.

"It will belong to Noel one day," she said. "Along with all my things."

Kelly accepted this piece of information with a tentative smile and a half nod.

"Noel was not like other boys," Mrs. DeLacey continued. "He was always gentle, sensitive, the complete opposite of his father, a macho football player, deceased at fifty of a heart attack."

Kelly nodded and tried for the sympathetic look she felt was expected.

Then without preamble, Mrs. DeLacey proceeded to instruct Kelly on the care and feeding of this "genius" son of hers, and the accommodation of his differences.

"I have always known," his mother said, "that Noel was different, that he has precious and precocious gifts and God-given talents and taste. He decorated this apartment. Isn't it exquisite?

"He always seemed intuitively to 'know' things." She studied Kelly a moment before she said, "You have helped him realize these talents. Now he is feeling the pressure of his destiny as a fountainhead of creative beauty. He needs sympathetic understanding and support, which he has found in you."

Rendered mentally openmouthed by these unsolicited confidences, Kelly felt a growing sense of outrage at the direction the discourse was taking. She had shed her gloves and was wearing Gary's mother's sizable diamond on the ring finger of her left hand, certainly within view of her hostess, who rattled on. Kelly had been lifting her teacup with her right hand. Very deliberately she raised it in her left and veritably flashed this "search light" into Mrs. DeLacey's eyes. It in no way changed the direction or content of Noel's mother's theme. Rather it amplified it.

"He loves you, Kelly," Mrs. DeLacey continued, "deeply, for what you have done for him. As his mother, I beg of you, please do not take yourself away from him now when he really needs you. He is my son. You cannot know what that means or what it means for a mother to turn over her son to another woman. He has spoken to me of you as he has never spoken of another woman. You are now the custodian of his God-given genius. For its future bloom and its beneficent impact on the world, you bear a responsibility."

This gratuitous assignment tripped the round bell in Kelly's psyche. The gloves now came off. "I bear a responsibility?" she exploded. "All I did was borrow a few lamps and climb a utility pole. Where does that make me a caretaker of your son? I am not responsible for his past or continued success or future."

"But he thinks you are," Mrs. DeLacey confidentially insisted. "You were his second believer. I, his mother, was his first. You will be here longer than I."

That thought gave Kelly pause. Did Noel's mother have a terminal illness? Did she have premonitions? What other reason could there be for shifting responsibility for Noel's welfare?

Kelly did not stay for his return. Mrs. DeLacey's full disclosure was followed by a discernible loss of rapport. With Kelly's blunt flashing of the ring that signified her engagement, there did not seem to be much more to talk about. So after a hollow exchange of amenities, she left, but not before Mrs. DeLacey captured Kelly's left hand for an instant and stole a close-up view of her engagement ring.

"What a beautiful solitaire! Forgive me, dear, but I couldn't help but notice it. An old-fashion square-cut diamond, in such good taste. They are becoming popular again."

Home in an empty house, Kelly felt depressed and called Gary. There was no answer.

An hour later Noel called. He was on a high. "Kelly, my dear sweet friend, I am so very sorry, but it was an important meeting. Midas has big plans for *Joey*. Pavel was there. He's the top boss. They want me to reshoot parts of it with a bigger budget. Isn't that nice?"

"How did you get along with mother?"

"I didn't."

"What?"

"I bombed. We didn't get along at all."

"Kelly! Are you serious? She did rave about you. Said you were a young lady of great charm and character. Said she never expected to meet anyone like you in Hollywood. She said you were refreshing."

Kelly sniffed. "You want the truth? Your mother proposed to me, for you. And I turned her down because I am presently engaged to be married to a wonderful someone else. How does that make me charming and refreshing?"

There was a long silence before Noel spoke again. This time with an unfamiliar note of firmness in his voice. "Let's throw out everything that's happened up to now and get back to fundamentals. I offered you a job when I flew up to Montana. The job is still open. It pays six hundred dollars a week. Do you want it or not?"

Kelly rocked side-to-side in her chair in animated frustration. "How can I take a job here? Don't you understand, dear Noel DeLacey, that I am only here until Pop's health improves?"

Noel replied, "I don't care if it's a day, a year, or forever Kelly, I want you near me on whatever terms you declare, for the moments you can spare."

There was a long silence until Noel's voice came again, "Kelly? Kelly? Hello? Hello?" She hung up.

The next day as she opened her mail she made the decision to take Noel's temporary job offer and told him so. She immediately experienced a mood swing and asked herself, *Now, what did you do that for?*

To which she answered, *To pay bills.*

But it bugged her. She had never within memory availed herself of the traditional woman's prerogative to change her mind, a privilege her brothers dubbed, 'Sissy.'

She decided to honor her word, take the temporary job with Noel, but what would she tell Gary? She started a letter: Dear Total Possessor of My Love . . .

She stopped writing and stared at the page, then crumpled and threw it into the wastebasket. The new page suffered the same fate. Finally she picked up the phone and dialed the ranch number.

Chapter Eighteen

Gary's voice brought his presence vividly into the room. The depth of its heart tug was scary. Momentarily unpoised, she hid that in banter. "What are you doing, sitting by the phone? Who were you expecting a call from?"

"Kelly!" he joyously whooped. "When are you arriving?"

She ducked that question with a question. "How is everything? How is your mother?"

"She's fine. When are you coming back?"

"And the horses? How is my sweetheart, Dancer?"

"He's fine."

"And the dogs?"

Gary's responses were verging on testy. "The dogs are fine, the horses are fine, my mother is fine. Everybody is fine around here except me."

"Aw, poor baby. What'sa matter?"

"You know very well what'sa matter. I need you."

"I just wanted to hear you say it."

"So when are you arriving?"

"That's what I want to talk to you about. You see, I had to make a decision today. Pop's health is still sort of up and down. Some problems are dragging on, and Noel, you remember Noel?

"Well, he asked me to help him with his post-production work on *Joey* while I'm here anyway just waiting around. It would be purely a business arrangement and only for the time I would be here. The money is good and I do need to do something to support myself."

"Now wait a minute," Gary broke in, "If you need money—"

"Please, Gary," she stopped him. "Please don't be difficult or take this as a cry for help. It's just part of tidying up my life before I come to you. Please don't worry. This is something I must do to insure our happy life together."

The talk went on, but in the end she prevailed, and Gary grudgingly accepted her decision.

Chapter Nineteen

The breakfast dishes shoved aside on the Hunnicutt ranch-house kitchen table made room for *Speed Horse Stallion Register* and a stack of horse breeding reference books so that Gary and his mother could more authoritatively debate the merits and demerits of various combinations of equestrian bloodlines.

This quest for speed afoot had been going on virtually since his father's death, when Gary quit school to help his mother run the cattle business.

Ten years prior, at seventeen, ranch born and bred with more guts than brains, Gary had reached that age with the fixed notion: there wasn't a horse ever born that he couldn't ride.

To prove himself, he had to have a go at the rodeo circuit. Here he learned that while the camaraderie, the free-flowing "pigeon blood" parties, the fights, and the fleeting romantic conquests made fond memories, it was no way to get rich. Except for consolation gas money, the loser's take was the broken bones that went with the territory.

After two seasons of Gary's rodeo career, his father, "Big John" Hunnicutt, decided it was time for more "book" learning and decreed his son's enrollment in the University at Missoula. Here, besides brain exercises, Gary picked up the latest scientific approach to beef production and marketing, plus a smattering of general knowledge. He had started his junior year when he got the news that his father had died while breaking a feisty colt that reared and fell on him.

Gary grieved while nursing the ironic thought: Better his father should have gone to college and left the horse breaking to him. So Gary quit school and assumed his father's role, helping Marge run the ranch.

In need of a dream to break the monotony of daily routine, they took a shot at breeding a quarter horse fast enough to qualify for the Rio Dosa. It was a "shoot-the-moon" challenge, requiring just the right blend of thoroughbred for speed and quarter for quickness; chancy, but irresistible. The winner collected half a million dollars.

To date, they had not even come close to qualifying, but with each foal there was the lift of hope that this might be the one! If it failed, the result was still marketable and the time invested not a total loss since Gary had developed a talent for "cooling down" rejected track candidates and turning them into saleable cutting horses.

On this particular morning, Gary was harboring a quiet excitement—he had hatched a ploy that needed Marge's blessing.

Their six-year-old sorrel brood mare, Princess Pat, a direct descendant in the illustrious "King Fritz" line, was due to be bred. The significant presence of thoroughbred in her lineage made for an intriguing gamble.

Standing at stud at a ranch near Helena was Sergeant York, a great-great-grandson of that sensational quarter horse, Go Man Go.

As Gary perused the promotional flyer he began to get that tickle in the heel of his right hand near the base of his thumb that told him great things were about to happen. "A natural," he enthused to Marge.

"He's right here on our doorstep. We don't have to haul her half way to hell and back to get bred."

"What's the stud fee?" Marge wanted to know. When Gary told her, Marge exploded. "Five thousand dollars! Are you crazy?"

"That's the sticker price," Gary quickly countered. "You know we can deal. Give them a piece of the get."

Marge fixed him with a hard glare. "Listen, sonny boy," she began, "Nobody gets given a piece of my mare's 'get.' I don't need partners. That's a shortcut to the loony bin. I don't share well. You ought to know that. There's three things I never share: a man, a horse, or a toothbrush. Remember that!" On this exit line, Marge rose and headed for the kitchen sink.

Gary's silent scowl followed her progress. He returned his attention to the stack of reference books on the table and idly flipped through the massive *Stallion Register* before slamming it shut with sufficient force to turn his mother's head.

She watched him rise, kick a chair out of the way, and stalk stonily out the kitchen door. She read her son's movements. *Now he's mad again, and I guess it's my fault again.* Some days Marge wished she had never seen Kelly Ryan, much less invited her to stay at the ranch. Her son's past enthrallment with Billie Jean seemed at this moment easier to bear than the ongoing prickly moods Gary had fallen into since Kelly's departure.

The dogs announced a caller.

A look out the window identified the visitor through his ten-year-old rattle-de-bang truck. It was the Indian, Richard Lightfoot.

Wonder what he wants, Marge pondered as she watched him approach.

Chapter Twenty

When Richard Lightfoot was twelve, living with his uncle, Johnny Sunshine, in an ancient tin-roofed, rock-and-adobe dwelling on the shores of Flathead Lake, he found in his uncle's meager library a tattered copy of *The Life of Jim Thorpe*.

Between chores, helping his uncle in his occupation of fishing guide, Richard had read and reread the book so many times he could recite it from memory.

He gloried in the verification that a poor Indian boy like himself could rise from poverty to world renown! He was inspired to emulate Thorpe.

However, not being gifted with Thorpe's athletic prowess and encountering enrollment problems at Haskell and Carlisle Indian Schools after completing his grammar and high school education at the Kicking Horse Reservation School, he made his way, thanks to an Indian scholarship grant, into the University at Missoula.

Here, with a drive fueled by his passion to do something not only for himself but also for his people, he studied law.

Gary Hunnicutt had been enrolled in the university during the same period, but because their pursuits did not coincide they never met. It was several years later that Richard's wife Redwing, a Showlo girl working as a part-time domestic for Marge, brought them together.

While militating against Slade's gambling operation, which he openly charged with stealing money from the Indians, Richard Lightfoot's truck was blown up with him in it.

At Redwing's supplications, Gary visited her husband in the hospital. This was the first meeting between the two men. Subsequently, they became friends.

Seated together on this morning at the Hunnicutt kitchen table sipping Marge's fresh-brewed coffee, Gary and his mother waited for their visitor to open up.

Looking across the table, what they saw was a slim-bodied young Indian with a thin sensitive mouth, straight black hair, cut long, an aquiline nose, and black eyes that flashed with a zealot's fire.

Out of respect for his chosen legal profession, he wore for all formal public appearances, and this was one, his Sunday best: a dark broadcloth suit, white shirt, collar secured with a turquoise and silver-trimmed leather thong. His hat was black, flat-brimmed, pristine, crown unpinched, shaped precisely as it was when it came out of the hatbox at the Indian store. He was shod in seasoned but freshly polished boots and walked with the aid of a cane. He carried an ancient briefcase, from which he extracted dog-eared legal documents to support his arguments, accenting the action with flashing eye contact.

On this occasion, the Indian fished out two freshly printed campaign flyers, which he slid across the table. "In case you haven't heard," he announced, "I'm running for tribal chief against my grandfather, and I'm asking for your support."

They had heard the rumors but were puzzled at what he meant by "your support" since they were not Indians. They were aware that Richard's senile grandfather, Chief Shaggy Bear, the incumbent, had been a long-standing embarrassment to his grandson and concerned members of the tribe. The chief was not in appearance or demeanor what would pass for "presidential" or chief executive timber in any league. He was simply the oldest living member of the tribe, of which Slade had taken total control, using the ancient venal persuasions of wampum, firewater, and young squaws. Small in stature, his little face peering out from under the towering mass of feathers of a Sioux war bonnet was comical. When he clowned a war dance chant in his bearskin robe, the animal's head and teeth snarling from his backside, the picture-snapping tourists found him hilarious.

With Chief Shaggy Bear in his pocket, Slade bought the tribal council. Then with the advice and consent of his banker, George Mayfield, they proceeded to make the casino their personal money cow.

Richard Lightfoot put down his coffee mug, extracted from his briefcase a stapled sheaf of documents, and flipped them open to a flagged page. "This is from," he read, "Public Law 106-479, October 17, 1988 - 102 Statute 2467, an act to regulate gaming on Indian Lands."

He exchanged significant looks with Marge and Gary before continuing. "There follows a lot of legalese," he explained, "describing the makeup of the Indian Gaming Commission — three members to be appointed by the president and the secretary of the interior before it gets down to the nitty gritty." Here he resumed reading.

"Whoever, being an officer employee, or individual licensee of a gaming establishment operated by, or for, or licensed by an Indian

> *Tribe pursuant to an ordinance or resolution approved by the National Indian Gaming Commission, embezzles, abstracts, purloins, willfully misappropriates, or takes and carries away with intent to steal, any monies, funds, assets, or other property of such establishment of value in excess of 1,000 dollars, shall be fined not more than $1,000,000 or imprisoned for not more than twenty years - or both."*

The Indian lifted his gaze to look wordlessly at his listeners.

Gary and his mother well knew the history of their guest, as did every resident of the area and his microcosmic "Man of La Mancha" fight against evil. Everyone knew substantial profits were being generated by Slade's casino.

Everyone knew none of this money had resulted in tribal benefits, medical care, or schools for the Indians. Everyone knew that when Richard Lightfoot began asking questions, his truck was blown up, but nobody did anything about it.

"How can we help you?" Gary asked.

Lightfoot laid down the papers he held in his hand and extracted another document from his briefcase. "Through persistent nagging and begging Indian Affairs, I have finally obtained from Washington an edict mandating a free election for chief of the Showlo Indian tribe. Slade has been officially served and has agreed to comply with the order, election date to be set. However," he added significantly, "the polling place will be the tribal council chamber in the casino.

"What I need now is a commitment from a volunteer poll watcher, a respected citizen, to monitor the balloting and insure my getting an honest count." Lightfoot stared Gary in the eye and waited.

Gary took his stare for a beat, grinned, and exchanged a look with his mother before responding. "Richard," he began, "I like your style. More than that, I like your guts, but, with all due respect, you are not exactly an advertisement for successfully bucking a stacked deck."

The Indian's eyes flashed in anger. He slammed his hand on the table and rose abruptly. "Slade is not only stealing the tribe blind, he is corrupting the neighborhood. Our young men are being hooked on drugs, our girls tempted with easy money to become prostitutes. Somebody has to stop him!"

Short-fused, feeling he had been rebuffed, he began to gather his papers. "I may be in this alone, but in spite of what they did before, I'm still here and running. My old truck they blew is still here and running and we're going to keep on running until we run these people off the reservation. It's either them or us." His papers stowed in his briefcase, he snapped it shut and moved to go.

Gary quickly rose and laid a hand on his arm. "Whoa, now don't run off mad. I haven't said no, yet. But right off, I don't figure I'd be too welcome at Slade's place. Last time there, we had words and I fed him a knuckle sandwich. He tends to remember those things."

Lightfoot, controlling his disappointment at getting no immediate commitment from Gary, picked up his briefcase as he muttered a, "Yeah, well." He called to Marge in the kitchen. "Thank you for the coffee, Mrs. Hunnicutt."

She came out drying her hands on a kitchen towel. "You're welcome anytime, Richard. Have a good day."

"You too." The amenities were hollow.

Richard turned to go, then stopped as he remembered something. "I took the liberty of unloading your mailbox on the way in. The mail is in the truck."

Gary responded with, "Thanks," and they walked in awkward silence to the Indian's truck. Gary studied the vehicle curiously. It had been painstakingly rebuilt by its owner after the explosion, as had its owner's body. It was a miracle both had survived.

Richard got in and handed out the mail.

Gary took it and said, "Thanks again." There was another awkward moment during which Gary said, "Take care."

Richard replied, "You too," and hit the starter button. As Gary watched the truck rattle out toward the highway, he felt low. He could and should have handled the encounter in much smoother style, but he had been totally unprepared for the Indian's surprise request.

The day had started badly with his mother's blunt veto of his horse-breeding ideas, followed by the downer of the Indian's visit. Seeking a lift, he shuffled quickly through the mail in hopes of finding that exciting faintly perfumed envelope with the familiar handwriting featuring generous loops that could only come from one person, but there wasn't any. Just junk mail and bills.

Marge watched through the kitchen window Gary's reflective, pebble-kicking progress back toward the ranch house. She read her son's diffident mood as he shuffled hopefully through the mail again. She felt a twinge of regret at having reacted so violently to his breeding suggestion.

On the Richard Lightfoot plea, part of her would have liked him to react like the stand-up guy his father had been, while another voice quietly applauded his caution. These matters were dwarfed by what she sensed was becoming Gary's sleep-robber. No letter from Kelly. There had been none since the phone calls about her taking the job with Noel.

Buddy Ebsen

Chapter Twenty-One

Seated at the reception desk of Noel's impressive business suite, Kelly found that her new temporary job security afforded her repose to study people.

She never realized she had so many close friends out of work wishing her success in her new job, or that there were so many actor's agents who made a professional rite of cultivating new secretaries, if that was what she was. She wasn't sure.

Having become a contact apparently of some potential, Kelly began to receive personal approaches from enterprising males. These she parried with a breezy, "Thanks very much, but no thanks, I've been took."

Men, she mused, come in various degrees of masculinity. There had been her father, anchored at the base of the gender spectrum, totally insensitive to a woman's point of view. Arching toward an imaginary apogee that separated the sexes, there were at various stations, Junior, Father Hennesy, Kevin, Duke, and hopefully, on the male side at the apex, Noel. Gary was completely off this chart.

Confronted by his quietly overpowering masculinity, the tomboy in Kelly had beaten a hasty retreat, taking refuge for the first time of her life in femininity. Gary made her feel like a woman, a scary new sensation with which she had not yet come to terms.

She returned to pondering her boss, this sensitive young charmer, Noel DeLacey, whose consuming surrender to what is beautiful formed the compelling element of his charm. Theirs was a friendship Kelly had as yet been unable to define.

As the *Joey* postproduction work progressed, seeing her name among the film credits as production assistant excited Kelly with a new pleasurable feeling of worth, in having Noel so freely acknowledge her part in his success. In many instances, the 'whisper' in Hollywood is more potent than fact.

Regarding Noel and *Joey*, the talk was reminiscent among old hands, of Garson Kanin's initial success with *A Man To Remember*, a hundred-thousand-dollar "sleeper" that elicited from his boss, Sam Goldwyn, the Goldwynism, "Dot kid's a clever genius."

Their names coupled with Midas, the intriguing reclusive European money source, Noel and Kelly's entrance turned heads at the "in" bistros. The deference shown them by maître d's was a new experience for Kelly. How could she not enjoy it?

Noel wore well the affluence supplied by his backers, dispensing it with princely charm and the assurance of one "to the manor born." Because of his ingratiating style, his prospects rose on a thermal of promise.

Though there was in their relationship a unique shyness, a non-acknowledgement of sex, there was a simpatico, a comfortable intuitive sharing of feelings and humor that made for pleasant good company, almost like with a girlfriend, but with an added something as yet unisolated.

One evening, a week on the job, after a very long day fielding non-essential phone calls and "drop-ins" who had suddenly discovered there was an interesting new tenant in the building, Kelly was bored.

Noel had been out all day scouting locations for the *Joey* added scenes. It was eight o'clock, long after office hours, but Kelly had two important messages she had promised to deliver to him personally. So she waited. When he finally arrived with an apology and his infectious grin, he hit her with, "How would you like to go to a place I know called Luigi's on Melrose, among all those boutiques, where pasta comes al dente, without you having to ask for it that way, and the wine list will stack up well with any place in town?"

Kelly grinned back. "What are we waiting for?"

So they closed up the office. Luigi's was on Melrose near Carson, an area jumping with dining action, especially on Fridays. It gave Kelly a lift, after a long day holding down the office, just to be out among people.

The place was jammed, but Luigi's greeting was warm and effusive. "Ah, good evening, Mister DeLacey. It's good to see you again." He acknowledged Kelly with, "And such a beautiful *signorina—Bella Bella*!"

Kelly smiled her acknowledgement of the compliment.

"We are very busy tonight, but I have a table for you. Come." He led them through a din of conversation and happy laughter, through the dining room bustling with handsome young Italian waiters.

From the region of the kitchen beyond a glass partition there came, besides a melodic rendition of *Volare* from one of the chefs, the agreeably faint but enslaving aroma of garlic.

Luigi seated them at a somewhat secluded table, and Kelly looked around. The place was full of attractive young couples deeply involved in loving attentions, and she felt the sudden stab of longing. She wished she were here with Gary.

Noel had capellini with Luigi's special pomodoro sauce, Kelly her favorite, fettuccine Alfredo. Luigi suggested Sauve Bola, an unpretentious but highly agreeable little wine, just right for its role on this occasion.

By the time the espresso was served, they were sharing a luxurious sense of well being. Since Kelly and Noel's telephonic exchange that had led to the present status, there had been no further discussion of Noel's mother, yet her presence hung heavily over this meeting. Any conversation that involved her might be uncomfortable, but any conversation that did not, would read like an awkward deliberate avoidance of the subject.

The wine set the mood, however, and nudged them to a stage of their friendship when frank discussions of sexual orientation were not uncomfortable. After her third glass of wine from their second bottle, Kelly studied Noel for a long beat. Finally, she said, "Are you gay?"

Her line caught him in the middle of a swallow. He choked and convulsed into a spasm of violent coughs, which segued into raucous laughter that turned heads at neighboring tables.

"Kelly," he finally was able to say. "You are priceless." And he resumed his laughter.

"Don't give me bullshit," she flung at him. "Answer the question."

"Why?" he asked.

"Why? I'll tell you why. Your mother thinks you are. Furthermore, she thinks I should accommodate your gayness because you are a genius. Well, I've got news for your mother. I have another agenda. Now, answer the question."

"I will," was his studied reply. "But first you have to answer a question."

"What?"

"Do you mean totally?"

Kelly pondered that. "I don't know what you mean."

"Is it true," he queried, "that to be a great artist one must know from having experienced all there is of life before one can create works of substance that communicate totally?" He looked at her but did not wait for a reply. "However if this is so, how did the classic, *Red Badge of Courage* get written when Stephen Crane had never experienced a single day of war? On the other hand, consider Hemingway's intriguing discovery in *For Whom the Bell Tolls* that there is in all of us a little of something that there should not be."

The glibness of Noel's response suggested the thoughts had been gleaned, organized, and mentally rehearsed in answer to his own moments of self-examination.

Lying in her bed, she reviewed the dialogue before she fell asleep; Kelly conceded Noel had answered her question. The answer was 'Not totally.'

Buddy Ebsen

Chapter Twenty-Two

The following Monday morning, Morrie Rivkin's secretary called. Kelly was familiar with the name. As one of the ambitious young agents in the television department of Galactic Talent Representation, his name was constantly in the trades.

Through his secretary, Mr. Rivkin urgently requested a meeting with Mr. DeLacey. To accommodate Mr. DeLacey's busy schedule, Mr. Rivkin would come to Mr. DeLacey's office. This concession and the urgency were flattering.

Kelly set it up for ten o'clock the following day. He showed up at 9:45.

"Gee, that coffee smells good," was Morrie Rivkin's confident greeting to Kelly, working the coffee maker, as he stepped into the office.

"Oh, good morning, Mr. Rivkin," Kelly responded, caught slightly off balance by his timing. "You're early."

"That's my style," he laughed, "the original early bird." Kelly scoped him as she moved. Young, late twenties, personable, brash.

"I'll tell Mr. DeLacey you're here." She stepped briefly into Noel's office, re-emerged, and nodded to Mr. Rivkin. "Please come this way."

"Noel DeLacey," he began as he warmly clasped Noel's right hand in his, while placing his left fraternally on Noel's arm just above the elbow. "I've heard such great things about you. I ran your film yesterday. It's brilliant! Academy Award stuff if we can find the right category or a shoo-in for an Emmy if we want to go that way."

"Thank you," Noel responded warily. He indicated a chair, and without interrupting his flow of language Morrie sat down.

"I don't want to steal too much of your valuable time, but while looking at your film yesterday a thought hit me right between the eyes. It's a natural."

He paused before his next line, which was weighty with significance. "I just got off the phone with Sonny Dunlap's mother."

He let that sink in. "She is reading your script, and if she likes it, we've got Sonny Dunlap to play Joey for you." Morrie leaned back triumphantly, anticipating the laurel wreath he knew was coming.

Noel looked blank. "Who is Sonny Dunlap?"

Rivkin tried unsuccessfully to muffle his explosive response. "Who is Sonny Dunlap?"

He turned to Kelly as she entered the room with a tray holding a carafe of hot coffee, sugar, cream, and two cups. "Did you hear that? Who is Sonny Dunlap? Tell him." Bluntness had replaced some of his opening veneer of obsequious charm.

"Sonny Dunlap is the cute kid in that hamburger commercial," Kelly said as she set the coffee service on Noel's desk. "His real father is currently suing his mother and her boyfriend for custody of the kid and his money."

Kelly's Quest

Morrie turned to Noel. "You mean you've never seen Sonny Dunlap eat a hamburger? Say listen, when he takes a big bite of this triple-decker, turns to the lens with his mouth full, juice running over his chin, a piece of pickle stuck on his nose, you just want to hug him. Then when he swallows and grins and says, 'Yum Yum,' you could eat him up. 'Yum Yum.' It's caught on all over the country."

"Guys are saying it to girls. Girls are saying it to guys. It's a national catch phrase and Sonny Dunlap created it. Yum Yum! You know what that trade mark is worth in dollars?"

Morrie's pitch easily carried to Kelly's desk in the outer office. Her frown suggested she was not buying.

"Has he ever acted?" Noel asked.

"Acted, shmacted." Morrie shot it down. "The kid is dynamite, a million dollar personality. You'd be crazy not to grab him, that is, if his mother likes the script. Hey I've got an idea. We have some film on him from a remake of an *Our Gang* comedy series. Meet me at the office at," he looked at his watch, "one o'clock. I'll run it for you. We'll grab a bite and talk."

There was a long pause before Noel finally answered. "I'll check my schedule and get back to you."

After Morrie departed, Kelly carted away her untouched coffee offering and stood patiently awaiting orders. Noel's countenance bore a troubled, faraway look. "Well?" she said, finally.

"I may throw up," Noel said.

Rivkin was not Noel's boss, but when one of the hierarchies of a powerful business entity requests an audience, it is the better part of valor to accede.

At three o'clock, Noel returned from his meeting with Morrie Rivkin. He walked silently past Kelly into his private office and sat at his desk.

When Kelly could no longer stave off her curiosity, she joined him.

"Tell me," Noel began. "When you capture on film, something so precious that everyone agrees is brilliant, how do you avoid the 'improvements?'"

"You didn't like Sonny Dunlap?"

"Straw-colored hair. Blue eyes in a Mexican family? Come on," he disparaged.

"You could dye his hair," Kelly suggested.

When Noel did not respond, she continued. "Then you're not replacing Joey Martinez?"

"Not with Sonny Dunlap," was Noel's firm reply. After a long silence he added, "Or anyone else."

The next day Kelly had lunch at Planet Earth, a trendy new soup and salad bar on Melrose. While she lingered over her espresso, a girl stopped at Kelly's table.

"You're Kelly?" she said, "Noel DeLacey's secretary."

"Yes," Kelly replied, as she looked up into the clear gray eyes of an attractive, smartly dressed young woman in her middle thirties.

"I'm Joyce McKennsie, Mr. Rivkin's secretary. I spoke to you yesterday."

"Oh yes, I remember," Kelly responded quickly.

"I saw you when you came in and wanted to speak with you for a moment. May I sit down?"

"By all means," Kelly said, and made a chair available. "Would you like some espresso? It's very good here."

Kelly's Quest

"Thank you, no. I've finished my lunch."

Joyce sat and studied Kelly. "I've seen Noel DeLacey's film," she said. "I like it. It's good."

"Thank you," Kelly said, on behalf of Noel.

"What I have to say, I hope you will treat as confidential."

"Oh, of course." Kelly made haste to reply.

"But if you don't, it won't make a great deal of difference, since it is not said maliciously but only in a spirit of being helpful."

"I understand," Kelly said.

"Noel is young, talented, idealistic, and inexperienced," Joyce began. "He has no concept of the minefield he is walking into at GTR. There are basically two factions: the old boys and the up-and-coming crop of young agents, all fighting tooth and nail to increase their share of the pie. And it's getting to be a pretty big pie. Last year over a billion in commissions.

"Top dog, of course, is the founder, Manny Gold. In the new crop, my boss, Mr. Rivkin, is the front-runner and heir-apparent to top spot in the firm. His domain currently is television. He has personal contracts with several lucrative performers, notably Sonny Dunlap, for whom he just renegotiated a million-dollar contract with Heavenly Hamburgers.

"But making the transition from television commercials to the big screen via Noel's story, if it all works, would give Manny's client, Sonny, a chance to cross over to the big screen and the bigger money as the new hot child star like McCauley Cawkins. Make sense?"

Kelly nodded. "Dollars and sense."

"Then perhaps you can explain it to your idealistic boss Noel. No one is trying deliberately to crush his budding genius. The morals and M.O. of this business are very simple and easily understood. Maximize the potential in dollars. Translation—make money. End of lecture."

She rose to go.

Kelly rose with her and took her hand. "Thank you, Joyce. I do very much appreciate your," she paused and searched for a word. "Confidences, and assure you they will be strictly kept."

"Oh don't worry about that. I revealed no secrets, and if I did, I have nothing to fear." Then she added with a twinkle, "I know where too many bodies are buried. Bye," and she departed.

Chapter Twenty-Three

The limo Noel had ordered to take his mother to the airport had not arrived. Nervous, she had called three times.

Mrs. DeLacey had decided she liked California. So the trip home was arranged for her to close up her house in Charleston and hurry back to enjoy the elaborate dwelling her son had provided for her in California, to bask in the glow of his success, and have a hand in determining his future. However, none of this would be happening until the limo arrived and took her to LAX.

Noel was in a projection room at GTR looking at film of possible cast replacements. Since the limo driver was obviously lost, it became Kelly's responsibility to get Mrs. DeLacey to the airport. She had forty-five minutes.

A call to Noel's condo got his mother's, "Hello."

"Hello, Mrs. DeLacey. This is Kelly," she said. "I'm taking you to the airport."

"How nice," Mrs. DeLacey responded. "I did so much want to see you again before I—"

"Good," Kelly broke in, "we'll talk about it later. Now listen carefully. Next to the elevator button in the hall is a button marked superintendent. Would you please push that and have him take your bags down to the curb? I will pick you up there in ten minutes."

"I have already done that dear," Mrs. DeLacey said. "He is down there now waiting with my bags."

Kelly felt a surge of admiration for Noel's mother. "Good girl."

"He is such a nice man," Mrs. DeLacey continued. "He's from Atlanta; his name is Luther."

"Good." Kelly cut her off again. "I'll pick you up in ten minutes."

She made it in five. Noel's mother aboard, bags stowed, "Do you have your ticket?" Kelly challenged.

Smiling, Mrs. DeLacey whipped the envelope from her purse and held it high.

"Good," Kelly said, gunned the machine, and they took off.

"I'm sorry about the limo mix-up," Kelly apologized as they threaded neatly through traffic headed for La Cienega. "The driver got lost. Hope this isn't too primitive for you."

Mrs. DeLacey beamed. "It's refreshing. I've never ridden in one of these before, and you do drive it well," she added as Kelly did a jackrabbit start on green, swerving into an inside lane, pole-position, all set to beat the competition to the next light.

By watching the yellow in the stop light, counting the seconds, and flooring the gas pedal precisely on green, she got the jump on her competitor without two much tire squeal and easily made it past the next light, something he failed to do.

Mrs. DeLacey let go an exuberant rebel yell.

Startled, Kelly looked at her passenger. "Are you alright Mrs. DeLacey?"

"I am having the time of my life. Kelly, I love your style. You could have ridden with J. E. B. Stuart. Did you know he was my great-great-grandfather?"

"No," Kelly said.

"Very few people know what the J. E. B. stands for. John Euwell Brown. Did you know that?" My people were the Browns of Virginia. Did you know J. E. B. once rode his entire command completely around the Yankee army?" She paused to let that sink in, then applied the topper. "Twice!"

The rest of their ride to the airport was accomplished with more detailed Civil War history, and then suddenly they were in the midst of the bustle of baggage check-in.

Mrs. DeLacey was flying Delta first class to Atlanta where she changed to a commuter flight or "puddle jumper," as she called it, to Charleston. She had her boarding pass and seat assignment. It was twelve minutes to departure, too late for normal baggage loading.

Kelly laid her problem and a ten-dollar bill on the check-in porter, who was bright. He spoke briefly into a pocket phone, took Mrs. DeLacey's ticket and accomplished, unhurriedly, the tagging of her two bags. He stapled the claim checks to her ticket envelope, wrote boldly across it "Gate 72," handed it to Mrs. DeLacey, picked up the bags, and laid them on the spare seat of an electric cart that had appeared as if by magic during the foregoing.

"Gate 72," he told the driver, "you've got six-and-a-half minutes. Have a good flight, ma'am," he said pleasantly to Mrs. DeLacey and went back to his chores.

Before she helped her into the cart, Kelly took Mrs. DeLacey's hand in hers, and said quite sincerely, "Have a good flight." Then impulsively she put her arms around the frail, feisty little woman and hugged her.

"Kelly, you darling girl," Noel's mother said. "Thank you so much for everything. I look forward to seeing you when I return." She waved, and they were gone.

There had been in their eye contact more than the message contained in their words. Their game was not over. It had just gone into overtime, which reminded Kelly to hurry and move the Jeep before she got a ticket.

When Kelly returned to her workplace, Noel was on the phone in his office with the door closed. The morning's mail lay on her desk, so she began to sift through it. Besides the office rent and telephone bills, which were by interim agreement paid by Midas, there were sizable credit card charges, most from restaurants that were to be paid from the thousand-dollar weekly stipend Noel received from Midas. Midas also paid Kelly's six hundred dollar weekly salary.

If you didn't look further, Noel's cash flow was in balance and satisfied his obligations. What it did not satisfy, however, was the packet of invoices from Grandeur Inc. Decor, amounting to forty-seven thousand dollars and eighty-three cents. These bills, she correctly assumed, were related to his condominium.

Noel's inner office door swung open, allowing him to deliver a brusque demand. "Get me Boris Pavel at Midas in Zurich," he said and shut the door with more energy than was necessary.

Kelly's Quest

Kelly, a little miffed at his insensitivity, got up, crossed to his office door, and opened it. "You may be interested to learn, Sir, I got your mother safely to the airport."

"Oh," Noel said. "Thank you."

"You're welcome," she said, her formality a rebuke. She shut the door, returned to her desk and picked up her phone.

The international operator gave her Zurich information who then supplied a number for Midas. Activating it, Kelly got an English-speaking female voice with a blurred national accent. "Mr. Pavel is in Hong Kong. Who is calling please?"

"Mr. DeLacey's secretary in Hollywood." Kelly responded. "Does Mr. Pavel have a contact number in Hong Kong?"

The voice ignored Kelly's question. "What is the nature of Mr. DeLacey's call, please?"

"A business matter," Kelly answered.

"If you leave your name and number, please," the voice said, "I will give Mr. Pavel your message."

Kelly complied and hung up.

The door to Noel's office burst open again, and Noel stalked out. He paced the room biting the little fingernail of his right hand.

"No luck reaching Pavel," Kelly volunteered. "He's in Hong Kong."

Noel did not seem to have heard.

Kelly watched him with some concern. "Noel," she finally said, "are you alright? Is there something I can do?"

"Yes," he said before he disappeared into his office. "Get me out of this contract."

Kelly sat at her desk and thought about that. Abruptly she rose, picked up the sheaf of bills the last mail had brought, and walked into Noel's inner office. "How good is your memory?" she began.

Noel looked up from the position to which he had sunk deep in his overstuffed, maroon-leather desk chair.

Kelly continued. "Can you remember back a couple of months to Gary's ranch? You arrived in the helicopter and we had a talk. You made a brave statement something like, 'I am not so naïve as to believe there will be no rough times ahead.' Then you said, that is when you would need me to stand by your side and sustain your confidence." She charged on, "Well, apparently that time has come. First, I have a question. Did you discuss the *Joey* casting change with Manny Gold?"

"Of course," Noel said testily. "I've been on the phone with him for the last hour."

"And what did he think about the Sonny Dunlap idea?"

"He loves it. He thinks it's a masterstroke. It will make the picture."

"And what did you say to that?"

"I told him if Joey Martinez goes, I go."

"You delivered an ultimatum?"

"So?"

Kelly paced three steps across the room, three steps back. She faced Noel. "You are an idiot!"

Noel's face flushed in anger. "Now, just a minute, Kelly."

"You delivered an ultimatum?" She paused. "You never deliver an ultimatum until you have become indispensable! Are you indispensable?"

Kelly's Quest

Kelly was very angry now.

Noel backed off and wilted. "They are pulling apart something beautiful that I bled and sweated and shed tears over, something you risked your life over that everyone said was brilliant."

Kelly looked at him, compassion nibbling at her scorn. She indicated the invoices in her hand. "I have here bills to you for close to fifty thousand dollars. You don't have that money. Who should I send them to, your mother?" She dropped the packet on Noel's desk and walked out of the room.

After a while, Noel picked up the invoices, looked at them absently, dropped them on his desk, rose, and stepped into the reception room. "If anyone calls, I'll be in Manny Gold's office at GTR."

Without comment Kelly watched him go.

Buddy Ebsen

Chapter Twenty-Four

It was on the five o'clock news, not the lead story, since similar things had been happening with such frequency lately as to make it commonplace.

The lead story was about a terrorist plot to kidnap the president's daughter.

"Plane Crash! Eighty-seven feared dead." What followed got Kelly's total attention. "In its final approach to Charleston International Airport, Sumter Airlines commuter flight 2026 from Atlanta crashed in a corn field during a heavy rain squall today."

Stunned, Kelly intuitively jotted down the flight number. She checked it against what she had scribbled on her memo pad earlier. It matched. She put in a call to Sumter Airlines, but could not get through. She called Delta who confirmed the news report. There were no survivors. She tried to call Noel at GTR. They gave her the projection room. He had left. She wondered if he had heard.

Then Noel walked in, exhausted but with a victorious gleam in his eye. "You can forget Sonny Dunlap," he announced. "He's out of the picture, and you will never guess why. His mother, God bless her, did not like the part!"

He seized Kelly by the shoulders and delivered the line in her face. "Do you know what that means? We won one!

Eeeeow." He let out a crow of delight. "Too small, she said. The part's too small for my Sonny's debut on the big screen! Well God bless Sonny Dunlap's mother. Oh, incidentally," they had progressed into Noel's office and he sank into the welcome comfort of his overstuffed desk chair. "Did my mother get off alright?"

"Yes," Kelly said hesitantly, wondering how to continue.

"Good, the limo finally got here?"

"No. I took her."

"In the Jeep?" He laughed. "Mother must have loved that."

"Noel," Kelly began. There was warning in her tone. He caught it and waited. "I have bad news." She hesitated. Before he guessed at the news, all color drained from his face. "The plane went down?"

Kelly nodded grimly.

"Survivors?"

Slowly, Kelly shook her head.

Noel exploded, an impassioned denial. "NO!" Then added hopefully, "Are you sure?"

"I checked."

Noel could not accept the fact. He responded savagely, "Well, check again."

"I did twice," Kelly said.

Finally, Noel rose. He crossed the room to the window and stood looking out of it for a time. When his shoulders began to shake, and she heard his sobs, Kelly moved to him and took his hand.

At her touch, he turned and put his arms around her. All the strength seemed to drain from him as slowly he sank to his knees, taking Kelly with him. Then he broke down.

"What do I do now?" he sobbed. "What do I do? Tell me."

Kelly did not hurry her reply. "You go there and do what needs to be done," she said.

"I can't do that. I can't, I can't."

"You must." Kelly said calmly with compelling finality.

Getting Noel put together and onto a plane headed toward Charleston occupied most of the following day. It was accomplished by Kelly with the aid of the venerable DeLacey family lawyer, Col. Dabney Littlefield, with whom Kelly established a warm telephonic relationship during the course of the day.

"I was deeply moved," he said, "by Dolly DeLacey's untimely passing."

After Kelly informed him of Noel's distraught condition, he agreed to perform all the gruesome details of identifying the body and arranging for burial. "All that would be required of Noel," he said, "would be to sign the necessary papers and attend the funeral."

Once Kelly had succeeded in getting Noel to accept his role, it was just a matter of finding him some dark glasses and keeping him moving toward Charleston. The ride to the airport was in silence except for Noel's fragments of memories about his mother. "She never punished me," he said. "My father did once. He never did again after Mother punished him." Three times, he said, "Kelly, you are my strength now. I don't know what I'd do without you."

Having been an eyewitness to the vulnerability of humans to the random impact of tragedy, Kelly was cued into morbid thoughts. What if something unforeseen happened to Kevin? Junior? Pop? What if a horse kicked

Gary? Or rolled on him as one did on his father. Needing instant reassurance, she dialed the ranch. No answer. She vowed to try later, and to occupy her mind, plunged into the accumulated paperwork.

Midas and GTR, their secretaries alerted, had sent overwhelming floral tributes to the funeral, which needed acknowledgement. Three actors' agents had called with condolences.

Since *Joey's* re-shooting preparations were put on hold, Kelly's principal duties were to screen the rubber-banded bundles of incoming junk mail, file most of it in the waste basket, and generally tidy up the office. Among the old messages on the recorder she found two from Father Hennesy that had never been answered. She called his number, and got a recording.

A week after Noel's departure, Kelly was startled when he walked into the office unannounced. At first glance, in his dark glasses and subdued mien, he seemed a stranger. He said, "Hello," and walked through to his desk.

Tentatively, Kelly followed, studying him before she spoke. "Welcome back, Noel."

His acknowledgement was a preoccupied nod as he went through the accumulated messages.

Kelly lay on his desk two additional notes from agents requesting appointments. Then, since he had picked up the phone and seemed disinclined to converse, Kelly went back to her desk.

Noel, still uncommunicative, as far as she was concerned, continued to make phone calls.

Kelly felt snubbed, like a piece of the office furniture. She sat at her desk and mechanically shuffled papers, then began to burn. She slammed the papers down and posed to herself a question. *What the hell am I doing here?*

The answer was obvious.

She had mired herself in other people's problems to the detriment of her own welfare. That was clear. Was it appreciated?

Did Pop need her? He was up and about.

She had done her duty by her father. Her brothers did not need her. To Mrs. DeLacey, a stranger whose objectives were contrary to her own, she had been more than civil. This out of respect for her friendship and regard for Noel, whom she had, by his own testimony, helped achieve his success. Now, to cap her sum of frustrations, Noel walked out of his inner office, looking neither to right nor left, passed her without a word, and stalked out the door of the suite.

Stunned at his wordless departure, she managed an unanswered, "Hey."

She hesitated, then scrambled to her feet and charged after him. She made it to the elevator in time to see the doors shut. She watched the lighted floor numbers get smaller as the elevator descended. What had caused this crude change in Noel's manner? Was it because she had been the bearer of bad news? The recipient classically attaches some blame to the messenger. An inner voice continued to mock, *What are you doing here anyway, foolish girl?*

From the vortex of events spinning in her head, Kelly was able to grab and hang on to one recurring message, "Go to Gary!"

She tried all day to find Noel to tell him she was leaving. He did not respond to phone calls to his condo or show up in his office for an appointment with a writer who had been assigned to help him write added scenes for *Joey*. No one at GTR had a clue as to Noel's whereabouts or seemed too concerned.

There was an office petty cash account on which Kelly's signature was valid. The balance in the account was eight hundred fifty-six dollars and eighty-seven cents. Pro-rated at one hundred twenty dollars a day, she wrote herself a salary check for the four days she had coming and locked up the office. She delivered the key and a note to the receptionist at GTR and went home to start packing.

When she arrived there, Kelly found a small envelope taped to the front door. She opened it. The message read, "Urgently need to talk with you. Please call me." It was from Father Hennesy.

Chapter Twenty-Five

With no mother, father, or close friend to help her sort out the mounting complexities of her life, Kelly had found herself, since Pop's collapse, leaning more and more on the counseling of Father Hennesy. There had developed between them a relationship unconfined by the rigid bounds of spiritual custody.

As it pertained to Noel DeLacey, Father Hennesy felt a sense of responsibility. It was, after all, his stipulated penance that had keyed their meeting and now what had it led to?

When Kelly had in the past lightly confided to him with sardonic amusement that she had been targeted as a prospective daughter-in-law by Mrs. DeLacey, Father Hennesy had begun to examine his dual responsibilities as both substitute secular and actual spiritual Father to Kelly.

So he had done some investigating and done it well. It was a pursuit that took him into the highways and byways of the community surrounding him, the gossipy, trendy, tawdry terrain of "Tinsel Town," the world of Hollywood.

Father Hennesy was aware of Mrs. DeLacey's death in the plane crash. He had further been made aware by Kelly of Noel's subsequent zombie-like behavior. Kelly had confided in him her heart's desire now was to return to Montana and marry Gary Hunnicutt. She seemed headed toward a healthy future, yet some psychotic motivation in Father Hennesy demanded recognition for his investigative skills.

The phone was ringing when Kelly opened the front door. She picked up the receiver. "Hello?"

A voice said "Hello Kelly. I'm so glad I caught you." It was Father Hennesy. "Will you have dinner with me tonight?"

"Tonight?" Kelly was taken aback. "Why tonight?"

"It's important." Father Hennesy said. His friendship was special, and he was persistent. In the end, Kelly agreed. They would dine at the Moustache Cafe.

It was six o'clock. He would pick her up at 7:30. Time to shower and change. Thinking it over as she made herself ready, Kelly began to like the idea. The Father was bright stimulating company. The meeting would take her mind off her problems. Kelly felt them disappear down the drain as she showered. She was putting on her makeup when she heard a car stop in front of the house. Father Hennesy early? Kelly fidgeting as she glued on an eyelash. But it wasn't Father Hennesy. It was her father; Junior had dropped him off after the ball game.

"And how was the game?" Kelly sang out as she took a last look in the mirror.

"Terrible," Pop growled. "No pitching. Where are the Sandy Kolfaxes of today? All these bums know how to throw is a fat home run ball."

He gave Kelly the once over as she entered the room. "And where might you be going all gussied-up like that?"

Kelly gave her father a mysterious smile. "Out," she said.

Kelly's Quest

Pop sniffed. "Not with Terrance O'Malley, I'll wager."

Kelly shook her head.

Pop said, "I thought not. You really gave him the brush off, and such a fine young lad he is."

Kelly smiled. "My dinner date, Pop, in case you are worried, is a nice, safe, respectable old friend. You will see him in a few moments and I am sure, approve."

"Who?"

"Father Hennesy."

"Father Hennesy?" Pop's reaction was not explosive, but it had a "Sonny Tufts" flavor.

Kelly caught the inflection. "Yes, is there anything wrong with that?"

Pop ignored Kelly's question, gave her a searching look and said, "Sit down, Kelly. I want to talk to you." When he started for the refrigerator Kelly felt a strong sense of déjà vu. But he did not get a beer. He got out a carton of low-fat milk.

In obedience to her father's command, Kelly sat.

Pop set the milk on the table and began to talk. As he talked he walked. He stopped once and glared at Kelly. "You've got a lot of your mother in you," he began. Then he acknowledged, in a softer tone, "and I guess a lot of me."

He resumed walking. "People thought I was the strong one because I made the most noise, but they didn't know your mother."

He continued to stroll, spacing his thoughts with an occasional pause for effect. "I was an ornery cuss — fought with everybody including my father until he threw me out. Then I lived in a cold-water-flat in Hell's Kitchen with two other guys. Between us we paid six dollars a month rent. We worked on the waterfront.

"Hell's Kitchen was a rough neighborhood. Both my roommates got busted for broaching cargo. One did time. The other shot a pier guard and got the chair. I was headed down the same road when I met your mother. It was at a Saturday night dance at the Hiberian Hall. That was it. She took charge of me and made me over. She started by reconciling me with my father. We got married. In doing that, Mary got disowned by her own father. So we moved to California, and my Pop got me into the stagehands' union.

"I tell you all this, Kelly, because to my knowledge nobody else has and you deserve to know. Since my trouble I've spent a lot of time at night thinking. Maybe I'm not right about everything. Maybe you know better what's good for you. I hear your mother's voice saying, 'Let her go, Pop. Let her follow her heart as I followed mine.' It didn't turn out too badly, now did it?

"So, Kelly, I say to you. Thank you for coming back. You've got this cowboy in Montana crazy about you, and you about him. Go to him. There's nothing in your life you will ever find that is more important."

Pop stopped talking and received Kelly's tear gushing embrace.

"Oh Pop," were the words that came from her, in no way a measure of the fullness of her heart.

"Hey, hold it," he cautioned as he hugged her, "or you'll have to do your makeup all over again."

"Give my regards to Father Hennesy. I'm going to take a little nap now, and don't worry about me. Junior will be back with the pizza soon." And Pop disappeared into his bedroom.

Buddy Ebsen

Chapter Twenty-Six

The waiter at the Moustache recommended Coquille St. Jacque, which was an excellent choice, Kelly discovered. Father Hennesy had swordfish. They split a bottle of Liebfrauenmilch.

Glowing with anticipation of shedding all her accumulated worries and fleeing to the arms of her beloved, Kelly gushed on about Gary's virtues. The young priest listened paternally.

Dinner consumed, Father Hennesy looked at his watch, then suggested they go somewhere else for coffee and liquor. Kelly thought the notion a little strange since the dinner at the Moustache had been enjoyable. Nevertheless, she acquiesced but wondered about their destination. She knew the place he had chosen by its reputation as a gay bar.

The Jacaranda was an intimate recently redone room on Melrose in West Hollywood. In the low-ceilinged discrete darkness, stabbed unobtrusively by recessed lighting, they followed the pen-lighted path of the maître d' to a candle-lit table where they were seated. They ordered cappuccino.

At the piano bar, the keyboard and bassist combo segued from *Strangers in the Night*, to Just *One of Those Things*. As Kelly's eyes adjusted to the dark, she cased the room.

There were three other couples, two dancing on the parquet-surfaced floor area. One of these, apparently heterosexual, could have been just sightseers, except that the woman was "leading" her dancing partner. From her, Kelly got "the look," the "are you one?" examination. The other couple dancing was a "butch" type in a tailored suit, her partner, a voluptuous blonde.

Seated in a booth, just out of Kelly's view, was the third party. From there came the murmur of voices, with occasional giggly laughter. Kelly was by now well aware Father Hennesy had not brought her to this place to dance. That left her with a meager list of conjectures.

The combo had begun a rendition of "Some Enchanted Evening" when Kelly noticed action at the table in the booth. A man's figure arose. When he turned to the light, she knew that face. Then the name came to her. Martin Brice, Junior!

Martin Brice, Junior, the producer who had fired and blacklisted her for slugging his star Brooks Rutherford. He reached back to lend his companion a hand. The emerging figure belonged to Noel DeLacey. The two melted into a dancing posture, Junior leading, swaying to the music.

Eight bars into the number, the dancing stance became an embrace, during which Junior planted a kiss on Noel's mouth.

Had it been a stranger, Kelly's reaction might not have been as extreme. But Martin Brice, Junior!

As Kelly watched, she became aware of a compelling truth deep within her. The delicious Coquille St. Jacque she had enjoyed at the Mustache Café less than an hour ago was not going to stay with her.

Chapter Twenty-Seven

At an accelerating pace, hand over mouth, Kelly started for the ladies room. Thanks to the intuitive intervention and timely guidance of the alert maître d', she made it.

When she emerged fifteen minutes later, Father Hennesy was waiting for her at the door.

Outside, deep breaths of the fresh night air revived Kelly physically, but did nothing for her pain. She stood for a while at the curb staring dumbly at the traffic speeding by. Kelly was not a naive schoolgirl. She was Hollywood born and bred, Hollywood schooled, and had been Hollywood employed, so she was not unaware such relationships between men exist.

It was witnessing one that traumatized her. One involving, in her view, individuals so totally disparate in character.

Father Hennesy, silent, watching, stood at her side.

He was sympathetically feeling for Kelly, but not regretful. He had done the right thing in totally opening her eyes. Had he not done so, he would have felt guilty. The timing was the fruit of his preparation plus the luck of the draw.

As for Kelly, she felt pain and loss. Big tears welled as she turned to Father Hennesy's waiting shoulder.

His first kiss was compassionate, fatherly, and comforting.

What happened after that was the fruition of a time bomb, a delayed slow-fused reaction to the campaign of perfume, sexy garments, and provocative made-up confessions Kelly had once in her silly girlhood past used in trying to get a rise out of this new young pastor.

The kiss, innocent as it was, lit his fire. His embrace grew from gentle to fierce. If his actions were designed to take her mind off Noel, they were a scintillating success.

Kelly panicked. She struggled, but his muscled arms crushed her to him. He began devouring, open-mouthed kisses on her face, then her neck. She was totally under the control of this out-of-control male animal. "Father Hennesy, please," she begged. "Please don't do that!"

Desperate, recalling a kung fu defense tactic she had once learned in a gym class, she sharply raised one knee. It worked.

With a grunt of pain, Father Hennesy released her, bent forward and crossed his wrists over his groin.

Freed, Kelly turned and ran directly across the street, through traffic, horns, and shrieking tires, stumbling over the curb on the far side, she fell and skinned her knee.

Rising, she continued at a hobble since one shoe had been left in the middle of Melrose. She took off the other and found the going easier.

Twenty minutes later as she trudged east on Sunset, a black-and-white on prostitute patrol made a U-turn and began to trail her. The unit pulled ahead, stopped. An officer emerged and intercepted Kelly's course.

It was Homer Jones. He greeted her with shocked surprise. "Kelly! What happened to you?"

Kelly responded wryly. "Ever hear of date rape?"

"Really? Who did it?"

"He didn't. I fought him off. But it was nasty."

"You want to press charges?"

Kelly shook her head. "No. I just want to go home."

He indicated her scraped knee, now oozing blood. "How about your knee? You want medical attention?"

"No, Homer," she pleaded. "Just take me home."

"Okay," he said and taking her arm, gingerly escorted Kelly to the patrol car. His partner helped her into the caged back seat, then shut and locked the door.

She smiled ironically at this routine precautionary procedure. Her strength depleted, she gratefully sank back in the seat and watched the lights stream by.

She grieved briefly over the lost shoe. The pair had been new and had cost fifty dollars. She made a mental note to go back in the morning and look for it. As they started down her street, Kelly saw through the wire mesh cage past the forms of the two officers in the front seats, red lights blinking up ahead in front of the Ryan house. An ambulance!

It pulled away just as they stopped, leaving the lone figure of a man standing on the curb looking after it. Junior!

In a flash of omniscience, Kelly read the scene and knew it for the truth. Pop was dead.

No miracle this time. Pop had passed away, perhaps in his sleep. Later, looking back to track her true feelings at the time, Kelly had to admit to herself that mixed with initial shock and pain, she had experienced a sense of relief.

It had not been a surprise. Pop's unusual behavior when last she saw him certainly indicated a premonition. His insistence on revealing his beginnings. His description of his relationship with her mother. His sudden acceptance of Gary, whom he had never met. Kelly was quietly amazed that no tears had come. Then she remembered Father Hennesy's words during the crisis. "Relax Kelly. Remember, not your will, but God's will be done." She felt a sense of peace of having done her duty by her father and now being generously released, freed by him to find her own destiny.

She felt a desperate need to talk to Gary, a need to cling to someone. She called the ranch three times and got no answer.

The funeral was by Hollywood standards modest. Old friends and union co-workers, Doctor Mendell, long-time Ryan family physician attended. Kelly, Junior, and Kevin were the chief mourners. Junior's ex-wife and son were there. Also Kevin's wife. A new priest, Father Delany, conducted the service. The Homer Jones family attended, and Pop Ryan was buried in the Hollywood Cemetery next to the grave of his beloved Mary.

Chapter Twenty-Eight

As Kelly left the gravesite, on her walk toward the parking lot she caught up with Doctor Mendell. "Why are you limping young lady?" he asked.

Kelly had not paid due attention to her scraped knee and now it was infected and very sore. "Oh, it's nothing", she said. "Just a little scrape."

Doctor Mendell had been the Ryan family physician for as long as Kelly could remember, so their relationship was paternal. He shook his head. "With the kind of germs around today any break in the skin is not 'nothing.' I want to see you in my office for a tetanus shot in the morning.

"But I can't do that," Kelly protested. "I'm leaving town."

"All the more reason to tend to that knee," he commanded. "Call Glenda for an appointment."

Somewhat annoyed at the Doctor's insistence, Kelly said she would, but had no intention of complying. The next morning however, when she woke with a very stiff knee, the scraped part inflamed and oozing, Kelly changed her mind.

Glenda, Doctor Mendell's nurse, was glad to hear from her and expedited an appointment for ten o'clock.

After treating the scrapes, Doctor Mendell perused Kelly's file and frowned. Regarding her over his bifocals he charged, "You have not had a routine physical in over two years."

"Can't we postpone that?" Kelly pleaded, hating the prospect. "I'm leaving town."

Doctor Mendell ignored her protests. "Glenda", he called, "set up a complete physical for Kelly." He turned to her "When are you leaving?"

"Tomorrow." Kelly said. Doctor Mendell shook his head. "Not with that knee, you're not."

Kelly found herself back at Doctor Mendell's office the following morning. One day later she was there again listening to the results of her physical. The doctor breezed through the list: "Vital signs normal, blood pressure good, breast check no lumps."

Conversationally, as he restored her file to the folder, Doctor Mendell delivered, almost as an afterthought, the question "Are you happy about your pregnancy?"

The Doctor's words launched a shock wave in Kelly's psyche that clanged and reverberated through her being and robbed her of an immediate response.

Historically, her menstrual periods were irregular, missing one had not been worrisome. Two? Subconscious concern had persuaded her to submit to the physical. The doctor's question had rocked her, but not as much as if she had not recognized that there was such a possibility.

She had experienced symptoms of morning sickness, also evening, if you counted what happened at the Jacaranda. Now it seemed there was no question. "The rabbit had died." The news, coming as it did at this point in her life challenged Kelly's character.

She took stock.

She had received no letter or phone call from Gary for three weeks. She had called the ranch. No one had answered.

Trying not to panic, Kelly considered her options. The most desirable of course was to marry Gary and have the baby. If for any unforeseen reason that could not be accomplished, it was not too late for an abortion. The mere thought was sickening. Her religion, plus her own personal choice ruled that out. The third solution: Have the baby and raise it herself. She wondered if she had the courage to do that.

From the churning uncertainties in her mind, one bedeviling question prevailed. Would Gary want to marry her under the new circumstances?

She was endlessly plagued by the chilling thought. Had she stayed away too long? Had Gary gone the way of all flesh, back to Billie Jean? That night, Kelly tossed sleeplessly in her bed. She checked the time. Eleven o'clock.

She had called the ranch three more times without response. In a way, she was glad of that. If Gary or his mother had picked up the phone, what would she have said? She had not worked that out yet. She blamed herself, her preoccupation with her stupid job, for the lapse in rapport.

The message she had for them was delicate, something you don't just blurt out over the phone, especially after a lapse in communication.

Since she had made up her mind she would go to Gary and couldn't sleep anyway, she decided to pack. This was to be her second trip and Kelly hoped permanent move to Montana. The house would probably be sold, so she had to plan taking everything of personal value that she ever hoped to see again.

Because she was sentimental and the Jeep space limited, this was a problem. However, in the storeroom she found her mother's ancient empty wardrobe trunk, a key still in the lock. This she filled with clothes and keepsakes and locked it against the day it could be shipped to Mrs. Gary Hunnicutt, at the JB Ranch, Showlo, Montana.

That thought warmed her with an inner smile. On her second trip to the garage carrying bags, she became aware of a man's figure standing quietly in the shadow of the Jeep.

It was a heart stopper. When he moved into the light, she recognized Father Hennesy. He spoke quickly, "Please, don't be alarmed. I am not a stalker. I came to beg your forgiveness, Kelly. I am under control. Please, listen to me because I am thinking clearly now, more clearly than ever before. Call it soul-searching, but I know now that I can no longer serve God within the rules and confines I accepted when I took the vows. I can no longer be a priest. The demands of the flesh that, after all, I believe God, not the devil placed inside me are too strong. I must leave the church and serve God in other ways. But I know now I cannot do this alone."

He paused to let the words sink in. "I love you, Kelly. Call it carnal, call it bestial, call it human, for that is what I know now that I am, a human being with the desire to serve God as I have tried to do with all my heart and soul, but not alone anymore. I find I cannot do it alone. I need help — your help." He paused again. "I need you at my side to do God's work together."

Kelly felt an adrenal rush of dread in anticipation of his next words.

"Will you marry me?"

Kelly steadied herself on the fender of the Jeep. She was sure she was going to faint. On a confused compassionate impulse, she reached out to touch Father Hennesy's hand, and then withdrew it as from fire.

"Please, Father Hennesy," was all she was able to enunciate.

"Kelly," he began.

Her voice rose emotionally. "Please, please, please Father, don't say anymore." She turned away. Then said quietly "And go away, please go away."

After a long silence she turned back to him, but he was gone.

Buddy Ebsen

Chapter Twenty-Nine

It was midnight on Santa Monica Boulevard, traffic dwindling. A noisy dumpster moved along devouring the trash du jour.

As this rather marvelous mechanical creation charged up to a welter of overstuffed trash cans, the two gatherers hopped off and with maximum clatter fed the monster's yawning jaws until, with a gluttonous roar, it swallowed.

Vengefully slamming the dented cans into their curbside stations, the gatherers hopped the running boards and the creature moved on.

Kelly, in her jeep driving east on Santa Monica, pulled around the trash truck to turn north on Gower. The cemetery gates were open. Knowing well the route, she parked close by the graves.

She took the two fresh-cut roses from the seat beside her, left the jeep, and made her way to the head stones. There was light enough to see the wilted, previously deposited blooms. These she removed.

The roses, she gently laid one on her mother's grave and the other on her father's. Kneeling in the dew wet grass, she prayed. Rising finally, dry eyed, Kelly got into her Jeep and drove away.

Three months had elapsed since she had begun her previous trip north.

With a predetermined destination and seeking a more direct route, Kelly chose US 15 through Vegas and Salt Lake City to the junction with US 90 at Butte, then west to Showlo.

Driving on mental autopilot through the long unpopulated stretches she planned to make it in two days. En route she tried twice to call the ranch without success.

Since Kelly's preoccupation with her job, the once daily exchange of letters or calls had dwindled. She now worried about just appearing on the doorstep without a warning.

As she drove, Kelly's stream-of-consciousness was a river of swirling whirlpools, each sucking her deeper into previously unfathomed depths. She had had at times good reason to feel in over her head, drowning in events.

So much had happened so fast since she had knocked Brooks Rutherford's tooth out. Images flashed back as though her brain had snapped pictures and was projecting them for her now.

The surprised look on Rutherford's face when he spit out the tooth. Horrifying then, ironically funny now. Pop's tantrum. Noel's beautiful face. Pious Father Hennesy with his feet of clay. Martin Bryce Junior—"You're fired! Get off the goddamn lot." Marsha and Jerry.

Kelly had found a letter from Jerry in the bundle of unopened mail she dumped into the Jeep before leaving home. She opened it during a pit stop in Idaho. "Dear Kelly," it began. "After a talk with Marsha who cleared up for me the misunderstanding of the night we met, I found that I can't forget you. Couldn't we meet sometime and start all over?" Fondly, intrigued, Jerry.

There was his phone number. Amused, Kelly mentally commented *Wants to meet me again so he can forget me*, dropped the letter into the trash receptacle.

She thought of Pop and her brother Joe in his Marine uniform. The faces were whirling by faster now. Kaleidoscopic, new ones. Gary, Marge, her mother, Doctor Mandell - "Are you happy about your pregnancy?"— Pop again, mean, vicious.

The sting of his blow on her cheek. Pop contrite. His benevolent release of her. Kelly's mind rambled on.

Is life like a soap opera? Or, is a soap opera like life? Welcome to the next episode of Kelly Ryan, Girl Girl.

Here she was, in her Jeep, minutes away from the entrance road to Gary's ranch, this time under her own power, the two of them that is, since she now carried deep within her this, small living souvenir of their spontaneous combustive love making, a popular misnomer?

Strong, mutual physical attraction there had been, certainly, compatible chemistry and the magic of the moment, but was that love? There had been obvious honest commitment in Gary's proposal and hurt at their separation, but did he love her? Did he *really, truly* love her? And did she love him?

What was love anyway, and had she ever known it? Was Gary still of a mind to marry her? And the jackpot question. How would he take her BIG SURPRISE?

Buddy Ebsen

Chapter Thirty

It was dark when, swamped by this weird fantasia of doubts, questions, and fast happenings, Kelly's reverie was fractured by the ranch dogs' announcement of her approach.

Barking their intimidating fiercest, they raced toward her oncoming vehicle, challenging, as usual, this invasion of their space.

Once they picked up Kelly's scent however, they quieted down, content to trot alongside, panting open-mouthed, tongues dangling, escorting her in.

Kelly parked and looked around.

Except for the dogs there was no sign of life. The ranch house itself was dark, seemingly deserted, spooky.

Kelly called out a tentative, "Hello! Anybody home?" No answer.

She had driven a long two days on the road. Fatigue was setting in, and she was cold. Having had no success in warning them she was coming, it was unreasonable to expect a welcome, but she wasn't feeling reasonable. She was tired. For an instant she was sorry she had come.

Dismounting, she started for the front door and became aware of someone sitting in a chair in the shadow of the overhang.

Marge Hunnicutt, a rifle across her knees, her preoccupied gaze was fixed on something beyond Kelly, out there where the dogs were now barking.

Kelly turned. A half mile away, at the ranch gate, a car had come off the highway and started up the ranch road. The dogs were racing to challenge.

As they watched, the car lights paused, then turned back toward the highway and disappeared unhurriedly in the direction of Showlo.

"Hello, Kelly," Marge said, rising. "We haven't heard from you in a while. Glad to see you again." Her tone was perfunctory, her look fixed on the disappearing car lights. Kelly eyed the rifle. "Is anything wrong?"

Taking her hand, Marge led Kelly to the door, placing her fingers where she could feel two small, round holes in the trim. "Last night somebody shot at the house."

Kelly said, "Oh, how terrible."

There was silence as Marge focused night glasses on the distant highway.

Kelly's poise was leaking. Someone on whom she had banked to off-load her cares had just beaten her to the punch. She missed the former subtle female sense of alliance.

She read in Marge's coolness something disquieting. Was it hostility? Marge's opening line, "We haven't heard from you in a while," had been a dig, which smacked of an intrusion into Gary's and her relationship. And where was Gary? Marge had not volunteered this information. So Kelly asked.

"Gary is at Slade's place," Marge told her.

"At Slade's place?"

Kelly felt a grab of concern. "Doing what?"

"Trying to help Richard Lightfoot get elected chief of the Tribe."

"He's there alone?" Kelly asked.

"Except for Richard and his wife Redwing."

"Isn't that dangerous?"

Marge sniffed and jerked her head toward the bullet holes. "Not any more than hanging around this ranch house." Marge's words were delivered flatly, but Kelly read in them deep concern.

"I think I'd better go see if he needs any help."

"Don't be silly," Marge exploded. "What could you do?" Marge's reply raised hackles on Kelly, but her response was restrained.

"Don't bet against me," she said as she started for her car.

Marge followed. "Now wait a minute, Kelly. Hold your horses. You look exhausted. Rest a while. Gary's a big boy. He can take care of himself."

"Maybe," Kelly said as she climbed into her vehicle and started the engine. "But if he's going to be the father of my child, I've got to be sure."

Marge looked startled. "What did you say?"

Kelly shouted above the engine roar. "I don't want to raise any orphans." She gunned the machine and took off.

Marge stared after her, open-mouthed, until the red taillights disappeared as the Jeep turned off toward Showlo. "Stubborn brat," Marge voiced her frustration as she started back to the house. Her mind churned on the impact of Kelly's final words. "Was she telling me something?"

Tell, hell, Marge decided. She was shouting it. "I'm going to have a baby," and you, Marge Hunnicutt, possibly a grandson.

And there she goes stupidly rushing off into danger.

"God damn it to hell," Marge swore in frustration as she kicked gravel and cudgeled her brain for a solution.

Chapter Thirty-One

As Kelly raced toward Jack Slade's casino through the beauty of the night, her churning mind flung off perverse thoughts. How could such inspiring surroundings, instead of giving us only "men to match our mountains," harbor its share of evil?

Morality here, she concluded, was no better, no worse than what she had left in Hollywood. As she had once read in civics class, crime thrives in all places where "good men do nothing". Gary was a good man. He was doing something. He was in danger. It was her "bounden" duty to help him.

Slade's parking lot was jammed. Many vehicles, but no people. That was a break. Kelly cruised the lanes looking for Gary's truck. She found it near a side entrance to the casino. Double-parked near by, she switched off her lights and sat, planning her next move.

Several cars arrived. Two departed. She started to dismount when a pickup peeled off the passing traffic. It rolled tentatively through the parking area, paused behind Gary's truck, and then moved on out of sight.

Moments later it reappeared and pulled into the slot next to Gary's. Scooched down, out of sight, Kelly watched. There was light enough to read the logo on the door. "Slade's State Line Coral." Slade's truck! As she watched, the door opened and the driver got out. He was of medium height, dark skinned. An Indian. Kelly remembered him pumping gas. He looked around.

Apparently satisfied he was not being observed, he reached into the truck bed, carefully lifted out a weighty object and disappeared with it between the two vehicles.

As Kelly watched, a side door to the casino opened and a man's figure emerged. Slade!

The truck driver reappeared, had a short conference with Slade. Then Slade reentered the casino.

The Indian now re-parked Slade's truck a short distance away, got out, and melted into the darkness.

No one else in sight, Kelly eased out of the jeep. Moving cautiously, she checked out Gary's truck. Wedged under the left front wheel was this pancake-shaped sand-colored metallic thing.

With her key-ring flashlight, she read the stenciled lettering. U.S. M XV. She had never seen a land mine, except in newsreels as soldiers with metal detectors cleared them from the projected assault lanes for Desert Storm.

Cold sweat beaded her forehead as she assimilated this discovery. Marge's laconic words flashed back. "They're a rough crowd." Kelly's teeth clenched on an ironic smile. You ain't just flapping your gums, Marge. Then, heat took over and her sweat turned to steam.

Those sons of bitches are trying to murder Gary - Then the delayed thought – the father of my child! What do I do about it? Call the police? Hah! What police? Slade's security, armed, are his personal troops. So, what to do? Gary is in there somewhere. Find him and warn him?

Just the two of us against Slade's gang? Suicide! What do you do, Kelly, quickly? Her eyes went to Slade's truck parked safely, a half block away.

The cogs whirled and stopped on force majeure, Act of God. How would God act? Would He punish the wrongdoer? And how He would! How? Why, through His servant, me, Kelly Ryan, the force majeure.

Very gingerly on her knees, Kelly brushed the sand from under the land mine. Then with meticulous care to avoid contact with any part of the devise that looked like a fuse, she picked it up and headed for Slade's truck. As she clutched it to her belly, she thought of the baby inside her, inches away, and the stories she would tell him years later, of his adventures before he was born.

Carefully planting the mine behind Slade's left front wheel, Kelly straightened up and looked around. Satisfied she had not been observed, she began to consider her approach to her primary mission: to find and help Gary.

Buddy Ebsen

Chapter Thirty-Two

In the casino rear parking lot, Kelly found a motley crowd of Indian women, some shepherding children, gathered around a truck bed from which an attractive young squaw was addressing them via bull horn.

"How long, oh Honorable Women of the Showlo Nation? How long will you accept second-class citizenship in your tribe? How long will you allow yourselves to be ruled and degraded as 'squaws,' taken advantage of by chauvinistic males?"

Dramatically, she stabbed an accusing finger at the casino. "Sitting now in that council chamber, behind that barred door, are twelve men and a senile chief who are, once more, selling out your birth rights as our ancestors did for a string of beads and a jug of firewater. How long, oh noble Showlo women, sprung from a great Indian nation, how long will we allow this outrage to continue?"

Then, at a higher pitch, she lapsed into the Indian tongue, *"Chi no alla beewano baba Stan tay uni bah!"* Which was chorused by her aroused listeners before they started moving toward the barred door and in frustration, pounded on it.

Kelly felt instant sisterhood with this young feminist with the bullhorn. As she climbed down off the truck Kelly approached and introduced herself. "Hi, I'm Kelly Ryan. I like your style. Who are you?"

The young woman regarded her curiously. "Thanks. I'm Redwing Lightfoot."

"I'm looking for a friend," Kelly continued. "Gary Hunnicutt. Do you know him?"

The name magically captured Redwing's total attention. "Sure. He's in there now, backing up my husband, Richard Lightfoot. They're monitoring the tribal election. It's rigged, as usual, through the Council-holding proxies, and Slade's goons won't let us in to protest."

Kelly made her way to the barred door. She inspected the hinges. The Indian women impatiently rioting around her, Kelly, with a pair of pliers and a screwdriver borrowed from one of the Indian trucks, went to work on the hinges.

Seated inside the council chamber at a table cluttered with papers, Gary Hunnicutt scribbled on a note pad. He tore off the page, handed it to Richard Lightfoot, who perused it, then chalked on a blackboard next to Chief Shaggy Bear's name 167, next to Richard Lightfoot 200.

There was ominous silence from the twelve men seated in chairs around the table. Richard turned to his grandfather.

"Chief Shaggy Bear, these are the final results of the tribal election for Chief. Do you concede?"

The chief rose and beckoned to a burly pair of armed security guards who stepped forward. They dragged a burlap sack, its contents bulging. The chief smiled. "In answer to your question, my son, not before we count my proxies." The guards stepped to the table and poured out the contents of the sack, a blizzard of paper. The Chief smiled at his grandson. "Now Richard, do you concede?"

In Slade's private office, watching on a monitor with Billie Jean and Mayfield, Slade let go a victorious whoop and took another swig from the bottle of Jack Daniels he fondled.

"That ought to do it," Mayfield said smugly, while Billie Jean moved closer to the back of Slade's chair and slithered her arms around his neck.

As they watched the monitor and savored their victory, the back doors of the council chamber collapsed and the angry horde of Showlo women came pouring through.

Buddy Ebsen

Chapter Thirty-Three

"Son of a bitch," Slade exploded as he slammed down his bottle and picked up the phone. He punched a button and barked into the receiver. "Security!" He waited, then slammed the receiver down and demanded, "Where the hell is everybody?"

On the monitor, three security police arrived to quell the uprising. Seeming reluctant to use weapons on women, some of whom were their own wives, they were stymied particularly by one squaw wielding a tomahawk.

Slade picked up the whiskey bottle, took a long swig, set it down, and started determinedly for the door. Mayfield stopped him. "Wait a minute Jack. Where you going?"

Slade shook him off and crossed back to his desk. "I'm going to protect my property and kill the son of a bitch that started all this."

Taking a pistol from the desk drawer he checked the cylinder, pocketed the weapon, and again started for the door.

Mayfield panicked. "You're crazy."

Alarmed, Billie Jean grabbed Slade's arm. "Don't Jack," she pleaded.

Slade, with Billie Jean hanging on, was making progress toward the council chamber. When Mayfield saw his investment in Slade's casino dropping from sure thing to high risk, he prudently opened the back door to Slade's office, stepped out, and quietly stole away.

Slade, now free, rushed down the corridor toward the council chamber. He easily spotted Gary's tall figure above the melee. In Slade's mindless rage, spontaneous words tumbled out, born of festering grievances long bottled up in his murky subconscious. "Hunnicutt, you've bugged me ever since high school, but you're not going to bug me any more." He drew his pistol.

Kelly, in the parking lot, in the custody of two security guards, heard the shot. It hit her with a clutch of numbing dread. Gary! They had killed Gary!

She had thwarted their plot with the land mine. They had gotten him with a bullet!

The two security guards abandoned her to rush toward the sound of the gunshot. Kelly followed.

Chapter Thirty-Four

The melee in the council chamber, frozen into silence by the shot, was regaining its voice as people recovered and cautiously pressed forward.

In the corridor to Slade's office, a tight little knot of curious had gathered around a body. Kelly fought her way through the crowd to look.

There, blood staining a widening area of her blouse, lay Billie Jean. Gary knelt at her side.

When Slade leveled the pistol at Gary, an eyewitness related later, Billie Jean had rushed in screaming "NO," thrown herself between the two men, and taken the bullet.

Slade, shaken by what he had done, took two hesitant steps toward the fallen girl, paused and retreated uncertainly toward his office.

Above the babble Kelly heard someone shout, "Get a doctor."

With Billie Jean in his arms, Gary rose, turned abruptly and bumped squarely into Kelly. Uttering a perfunctory "Excuse me, I've got to get this lady to the–," his eyes widening in astonished, delayed recognition, "Kelly?"

Having already absorbed the initial shock of this bizarre encounter, Kelly held an advantage. Out of Gary's open mouth came a highly inadequate welcome for a girl in Kelly's circumstances.

Awkwardly indicating Billie Jean, he made a redundant announcement, "She's been shot!" After a hesitant step on his way, and over his shoulder, he said, "I've got to get her to a doctor."

They were gone, but not before Billie Jean, quite conscious, fluttering lashes, bestowed on Kelly, over Gary's shoulder, a lingering Cheshire-cat smile.

A buzz of voices invaded Kelly's consciousness. "Bravest thing I ever saw. She took the bullet meant for him."

"Must have been crazy."

"Yeah, about him."

Dazed, mouth slightly ajar, full of words that never came out, Kelly stood a while before she stumbled out the door toward the parking lot. She felt weak, drained suddenly of all the second-wind strength she had plugged into when she left Marge.

She found her Jeep and, for want of a refuge, sat in it. She tried to think, with no mind left to do that. From what she had witnessed, Kelly believed she was now the unnecessary extra wheel on Gary and Billie Jean's wagon. Billie Jean ruled—who needs Kelly Ryan? Certainly not Gary Hunnicutt.

To the questioning lyric "Have I Stayed Away Too Long?" the answer was obvious. Billie Jean and Gary were back together again, and Kelly had too much pride to stay and slug him with impending fatherhood—beg for love? Beg for anything? Not Kelly Ryan!

Searchlights stabbed the night. Two helicopters were orbiting the area when eventually Kelly started her car, released the brake, and rolled out onto the highway.

Buddy Ebsen

Chapter Thirty-Five

As Gary carried Billie Jean toward the parking lot, he concluded the presence of the two orbiting helicopters suggested Richard Lightfoot's long dedicated campaign for justice from the government had finally paid off. His conclusions were verified by the arrival of a fleet of unmarked surface units that disgorged bareheaded young men in dark suits bearing white identification clips on their lapels. As they disembarked and stormed the casino, Gary spotted a white panel truck marked with a red cross. The two alert medics automatically took charge of this first raid casualty. A cursory examination determined that Billy Jean had only sustained a flesh wound. Gary's relief was wreathed in gratitude for her impulsive act in taking the bullet meant for him. Satisfied the girl was in good hands, he left.

Inside the casino he found a phone booth and called his mother. Marge, who had apparently been waiting by the telephone, was brief, forceful, and to the point. Their first two words were spoken almost in unison. "Kelly's back."

"I know," Gary said. "I just saw her."

"Is she all right?" Marge wanted to know.

"I don't know. She's disappeared."

"Well, find her!" Marge commanded testily.

"Yeah, sure," Gary responded wearily. "I think I better fill you in on what's been happening around here. The Feds just raided the casino."

"Don't give me gossip," Marge commanded. "Find Kelly! And guard her with your life." She hung up.

Gary hung up, miffed and mystified at his mother's abruptness. Then he set about in earnest to find Kelly.

Through the casino, confiscating cash from the "change" cage and crap table slot boxes, the Feds moved systematically. They shut down all action, the only resistance coming from a sprinkling of diehards who, stubbornly continued to muscle the "slots," totally ignoring the raid in progress around them.

Meanwhile Slade, barricaded in his office, frantically completed the transfer of sheaves of hundred dollar bills from his wall safe into a briefcase.

This done, he pocketed his passport, reloaded the spent round in his pistol and slipped out the private exit into the night.

Here Tonto waited.

No Feds in sight, Slade ordered the truck brought up. He stood in the shadows while Tonto obediently trotted off.

Two minutes later, with a *chu-rump*, a *roar*, and a *flash*, the land mine blew. It lifted Slade's vehicle off the ground and dropped it on its side, a heap of smoldering junk.

When the concussion blast hit his cheek, Slade had instinctively ducked, muttering a fervent, "Jesus Christ!" Since the parking lot was now deserted, the raiding force busy inside, there was no immediate movement toward the explosion site. Slade used this moment to disappear judiciously into the darkness.

Gary heard the detonation and ran toward the sound of the blast. He had no way of knowing this event was a direct manifestation of force majeure with a "Kelly was here" signature. He looked, then left the smoking ruin and the hors de combat Tonto to the ministrations of a gathering Fed detail while he renewed his search for Kelly.

Buddy Ebsen

Chapter Thirty-Six

Charlie Sheldon knelt under his chopper looking for possible damage to the landing skids. Heavy laden, in the dark, dodging surface traffic, the "sit down" had been rough. So was the pressure of the metallic thing thrust into the back of his neck, and the voice with it.

"Crank it up, mister. Let's go to Calgary."

Because he loved life, Charlie, without turning his head, rose to comply.

That is when Gary, searching the parking lot for Kelly's jeep, came upon the scene. His reaction was an involuntary "Hey!" Slade swung around, his pistol pointed at Gary.

The release of the pressure on Sheldon's neck triggered his blind roundhouse swing, a glancing blow, but it deflected Slade's aim so that his "snap" shot went wild.

His second shot was aborted by Sheldon's karate chop on Slade's forearm.

Locked in a clinch, struggling for possession of the weapon, Slade's finger still on the trigger, a series of wild shots sprayed lead.

Gary had hit the deck to avoid the stray slugs. When he looked up, Slade, having broken free, was in flight, clutching his briefcase.

Sheldon, now in possession of the pistol, leveled it at his fleeing target. "Freeze, you bastard."

Getting zero compliance, he pulled the trigger. The hammer clicked successively on six spent chambers.

"Shit," he muttered, as Gary took off after Slade. His flying tackle dropped the fugitive. They rolled.

Gary was on his feet first.

They were in a peripheral area of the parking lot where the light was bad. But as Slade rose, Gary caught a glint of the knife Slade pulled from his boot.

Slade charged, attempting two vicious slashes. Gary saw them coming and dodged them.

Slade then lowered the blade to a thrusting position, the weapon, coming rapier-like, directly at Gary.

Except for heavy breathing and intermittent scrambling of feet on pebbles, the duel proceeded in deadly silence.

To sharpen his attack, Slade, now advanced in a crouch, continuously flipping the knife expertly from one hand to the other in the sophisticated style of the experienced street fighter.

With the switch in Slade's style, something came back to Gary about knife fighting, learned from a rodeo buddy, "No way Jose" Rodrigues, after a fracas in an El Paso bar. At Slade's next right-handed knife thrust, Gary, matador-like, side stepped the blade. As the knife passed daringly close to his body, he clamped his right hand on Slade's wrist, giving him a short unbalancing forward tug. By simultaneously lifting his left knee briskly against Slade's extended arm and pulling with both hands, as you would to break a stick, Gary broke Slade's arm at the elbow.

Slade bellowed in pain and dropped the knife. Gary picked it up.

Alerted by the gunfire, two Feds, pistols drawn, came running. Led to the scene by Charlie Sheldon, they were elated to discover they had nabbed the "big fish."

As they escorted their prisoner away, they encountered Richard Lightfoot hobbling in. For an instant, the Indian's eyes met Slade's in an eloquent look exchange—triumph over silent, sullen rage. Hobbling onward, Lightfoot found Gary and Sheldon examining the contents of Slade's briefcase. Gary indicated the money. "I guess this is something you could use. It's evidence that might put Slade out of circulation for a while!"

The Indian stared at the contents of the piece of luggage, with exhilaration born of the dawning awareness this represented the key to victory, the end of his tortured quest.

He took the proffered briefcase, snapped it shut and set it on the ground. Then with appropriate decorum, assuming the persona of the role he sought in life, he formally addressed Gary in solemn tones.

"Gary Hunnicutt, henceforth to be known to my people as True Eagle, you are my white brother. For your demonstrated friendship, may the Great Spirit keep and protect you, guiding your footsteps in the way you choose to go." Then he said three Indian words, and let his cane fall to the ground so he could use both arms to embrace Gary.

With a roar and a cloud of dust, the whirling blades raised, Charlie Sheldon's helicopter took off to be swallowed in a black sky, and its course marked only by the red and green running lights it showed.

Charlie and his passenger Gary had no clue as to which direction to go first in their quest for Kelly Ryan's white Jeep. Charlie remembered he had seen such a vehicle depart from under him as he came in for his landing. Since it was "by guess and by God" time, Gary, still somewhat haunted by Richard Lightfoot's benediction, and trying to tune in on directions from the "Great Spirit," said "try south."

Charlie banked to comply.

Chapter Thirty-Seven

When Kelly left Slade's driving south, slowly at first, aimlessly, she did not really know where she wanted to go, just away, far away from this place. Things were happening to her, unpleasant things, too many, too fast. She could no longer field them.

The world was ganging up on her. The lineup was unfair. She needed help. One more on her side, a protector, an angel. When she was a little girl she had a protector, her big brother Joe. When Junior and Kevin ganged up on her there was always Joe to take her side, to level the playing field.

Where was he now? A Vietnam MIA? Two wounded Marines last saw him mowing down Viet Cong, holding them off so his buddies could escape. That would be Joe, all right.

Was he dead? No one ever saw his body. Did God love him so much that he took him directly to Heaven? Like Jesus?

"Where are you now, Joe? I need you. I want to be with you wherever you are."

Kelly was not aware that, as these thoughts streamed by and tears streamed down, her foot had gradually floored the gas pedal. She was passing cars recklessly, driving too long on the wrong side.

Tear-blinded, except for headlights, she heard but never saw the oncoming eighteen-wheeler bursting around the bend, blasting his air horn. There was not room for three vehicles abreast on the two-lane highway.

The pickup on Kelly's right wisely braked out of the scene, but a brushed contact with the monster on her left bounced Kelly toward the shoulder where the Jeep left the road and rolled.

Chapter Thirty-Eight

Gary Hunnicutt's relationship with God, rather than man to Deity, was man to man. "As long as you don't deal me an unplayable hand," he told God, "I will respectfully go to church, and generally stand up for what I believe is right."

When he was up all night in Charlie Sheldon's helicopter, dropping feed to winter calves and their snowbound mamas, he expected a square shake if he and God were going to get along together. So far, his herds had survived. But now stakes were astronomically higher. This wasn't calves. This was Kelly!

Charlie, headset in place, had been communicating with his base and various information sources since takeoff. He flipped a switch on the police scanner, turned up the volume and Gary was able to hear.

"A #602 working on US 90 at the big bend between Nine Mile and French Town. Eighteen-wheeler and an off-road vehicle presently off the road and flipped. One casualty – female. Two units on the scene. Ambulance en route."

Charlie and Gary exchanged significant eye contact.

"I would say," Charlie said, "we are headed in the wrong direction." He waited.

Gary did not. "Go," he said.

Charlie banked the chopper steeply, and they reversed course.

Gary studied the chart. "The big bend, between Nine Mile and French Town."

"I know where that is." He took a pair of night glasses off the rack and searched ahead.

Fifteen minutes elapsed. There was no sign of traffic congestion below, which might have indicated the site of an accident.

Gary was re-consulting the chart when he felt Charlie's nudge. In the clear night air, far ahead, flashing blue lights were visible.

Five minutes later they circled over the accident site, already congested with the curious. The eighteen-wheeler, which had luckily avoided jack-knifing, was parked on the shoulder, diesel idling.

A state trooper, beside his blue light flashing unit waved traffic along while his partner, flashlight in hand, knelt beside an inert, blanket-covered body. He rose to clear space for the incoming chopper.

Blades still idling, Gary jumped and made for the huddle. It was Kelly all right. Sight of her bleeding motionless body hit him with sickening dread. A flash vision of a world without Kelly was heart stopping. He heard someone say, "She's breathing."

Please, God, keep her breathing, he silently prayed. Please don't take her.

There was no debate about protocol. After a hurried conference, she was carefully transferred to the gurney Charlie produced from the chopper and tenderly loaded aboard. With the dust-gusty roar of takeoff, the chopper with its precious cargo was on its way.

Charlie lost no time making radio contact with the control tower at Missoula. Half-hour later, they picked up the airport beacon and from there had no trouble finding the oscillating beam marking their destination.

The hospital was modern and ready with a rooftop heliport, spotlighted windsock, and floodlighted pad.

Two attendants, an intern, and a nurse were on the roof waiting. They very efficiently moved the unconscious girl to Emergency, where two nurses cut her out of her bloody clothing and into a hospital gown.

When Gary finally finished the paper work, Doctor Parker, the bright young intern was waiting. "You are?" He addressed Gary questioningly.

"Gary Hunnicutt," Gary said. "I am the young lady's fiancé."

"I see. I am Doctor Parker." He studied Gary a beat. "Well, the good news is that while Kelly has had a pretty severe bump on her head and is suffering from a concussion and numerous lacerations on her body, the x-rays do not reveal any broken bones."

Gary took a deep breath.

"The bad news is, her vaginal bleeding indicates she may lose her baby."

"Doctor Parker, Doctor Parker, report to emergency," the speaker summons interrupted. "Excuse me," the Doctor said. "I'll talk to you later."

"May lose her what?" Gary's delayed response never reached Doctor Parker's ears. Gary found a chair and sat down. "Baby! May lose her baby." That's what the doctor had said. Well! That explained a lot, beginning with Marge's cryptic phone message. "Find Kelly and guard her with your life," Marge had said. So she must have known. Why else?

Now that he understood the order, his whole-hearted resolve was, "Will do!"

Except for Gary, the hospital chapel was unoccupied. It was small, six pews, and an altar supporting two heavy-lighted candles. The stained glass window dominated by a full figure of Jesus, arms benignly outstretched in welcome to some lambs in the foreground.

On the right, flanking the leaded center pane, the Madonna and child, on the left the Magi. The quality of the artwork plus the low sustained organ chords coming from somewhere, combined to evoke a feeling of comfort, inspiring meditation.

Choosing the last pew, Gary found the surroundings powerfully conducive to a conversation with God. He had had, during his life, such conversations before, asking for one thing or another, mostly for less snow during calving season. But this one was different.

In supplication for Kelly's life, he, for the first time, addressed God from his knees. His approach was simple and direct. "Dear God," he prayed, "please do not take Kelly. I will obey whatever word you send me."

The nurse who opened the door to the chapel a half-hour later had encouraging news. Though still in a coma, Kelly's vital signs were stable, and the bleeding had stopped.

The news lifted Gary like a draft of potent elixir. He followed the nurse to Intensive Care. Hat in hand he tiptoed into the room. Kelly lay on her back, head heavily bandaged.

The nurse, after making some notations on a clipboard, said it was permissible for him to stay. When she left, Gary moved his chair closer to the bed.

Hurting vicariously, he studied the deep purple bruise discoloration around Kelly's swollen eyes. They stood out against the white cap bandage covering her head. He noted with gratitude, the strong regular heartbeat recorded on the display scope.

They had arrived at the hospital at 11:15. It was now 2:00 a.m. At 2:45, when Kelly opened her eyes, Gary was asleep in his chair.

She was puzzled. She remembered only contact with that monstrous barreling eighteen-wheeler, tumbling, a blow, sharp pain and blackness. Where was she now she wondered? In some crazy after life half-world, and what was Gary doing there? As she studied his face, almost as though he felt her gaze, he woke up. They looked at each other until Gary picked up one of her hands, kissed it and gently held it in both of his.

Then Kelly remembered something. Eyes closed she murmured, "I've got a package for you."

Gary's reply was gentle, tender, and amused. "Yes, I know."

"How did you know?" She tried to scowl, but it pained her, so she stopped.

"Does it matter?" He smiled.

She waited a beat before she said, "Are you mad?"

Unlocked by the words, Gary's rush of emotion born of hitherto untouched regions of his heart brought tears. "Am I mad?" he echoed. Slipping off the chair to his knees, he kissed her hands again and again, then gently her bandaged forehead. Finally tenderly he touched his lips to the sheet just above the baby. "Am I mad?" he whispered.

"Yes Kelly, I am mad, totally, furiously, crazy mad," Kelly opened her eyes wider, "about you."

Kelly closed her eyes.

Abruptly her hand clamped fiercely, possessively on Gary's, and then relaxed as a slow smile crept like sunrise across her bruised features.

EPILOGUE

Patrick Ryan Hunnicutt, at eighteen months, was a handful, a robust, redheaded holy terror, who perpetually "got into things."

Knowing he would need that drive and spirit in a rough-and-chancy world, Kelly would not have had him any other way.

Fortunately, there was Marge, ever eager to take him off her hands while Kelly herself took over Marge's job, helping Gary run the ranch.

In time, the event generally referred to as "The Slade Raid," became a local legend, glorifying the heroic actions of the Showlo women.

A bronze plaque mounted in the lobby of the casino memorializing the battle site, giving credit to Kelly and Gary for their help and making them honorary tribe members.

Richard Lightfoot, now tribal chief (and chief executive officer) wisely retained the Slade name on the casino for its exploitation value, now that Slade and Mayfield had been stripped of the property and the Indians became the legal owners.

With suspicion of narcotics dealing and tax evasion on top of a conviction for attempted murder, Slade was doing "ten to twenty" in federal prison.

George Mayfield charged with aiding and abetting, money laundering, and having turned State's evidence, was free on bail, but was, for reasons of self-preservation quietly paying off the parole board to keep Slade caged.

Billie Jean, fully recovered from her wound, went back to Texas, married a Senator and became the current Washington "hostess with the mostess".

From time to time Kevin sent clippings. One read "Hollywood Madam cleared of vice charges."

It had a familiar ring, the charges being dropped after the judge took a peek at the names and phone numbers in Marsha's "little black book".

There was a brief line in a gossip column about Father Hennesy leaving the church to found his own.

Then this:

Brilliant Young Director Dies

"Noel Delacy, who skyrocked to fame with his first picture Joey, and whose future held great promise, has succumbed to AIDS."

Kelly read the words compassionately, but dry-eyed. No person can ward off another's destiny – That, she had learned from Duke a long time ago.

There would be days in the bitter winter, when they used Charlie's helicopter to drop feed to their snow-bound stock, that Kelly would miss L.A., the balmy days, the beach, her job in the world's most glamorous industry, but would she go back? Would she trade her husband, her bouncing boy baby and her place in their lives, a place she felt was waiting for her to fill – the answer always – *No way*!

The cliff hangers, the near misses, the barriers overcome, that failed to thwart a destiny that stubbornly insisted they find each other, to be together, that now bound them, through sharing and overcoming obstacles, eternally together.

She had come to love the Big Sky country, its people and all it had brought her.

She even thanked God for Jack Slade's dirty gasoline that had opened the door to this fulfillment.

Hidden in every problem, she philosophized, is an opportunity. As she rode with Gary, rounding up strays, admiring his skills, loving as she had from the start, every move he made, she smiled at a recurring thought.

Everything in life has a purpose if you learn to use it.

Gary caught her smile. "What's funny?"

Kelly nodded toward the spot in the highway where 18-wheelers, toy size at this distance, were crawling by. "Could we put a marker there?"

"Where?" he asked.

"Where Jack Slade's dirty gasoline brought us together."

Gary looked off and grinned. Touched, he leaned toward her. But it was too late, a calf broke away and Kelly had taken off after it. Instead of helping, this time, Gary watched.

As Kelly furiously pursued the fugitive, she felt Gary's eyes on her, grading her performance, measuring it against memories of another rider.

The chase took them by a crude range holding pen, now empty, gate open. With a personally inflated value of what was riding on the chase, Kelly's subconscious addressed the elusive animal. "Alright, you stubborn little brat. I am going to pen you, no matter what."

The calf did a quick stop and reversed field.

"No you don't," Kelly muttered as she matched and covered the action. "You don't understand, little doggie, what's involved here. What the stakes are, but couldn't you give me one little break and cooperate? Come on now, go through the gate into that pen like a nice little critter, so I can shine for Gary."

But the calf did not. It broke away, Kelly chasing furiously after. "Damn you little monster," Kelly muttered. "Don't you understand? I have got to win this, to drive a stake through the heart of Gary's memories of Billie Jean Garner. I have got to drive the ghost of her out of his mind and earn the look I saw on his face when he watched her perform. I must, to insure our future."

After three wild breakaways, all contained by Kelly, the calf gave up and walked through the entrance to the pen. Without dismounting, Kelly approached, lifted, and closed the gate.

Not until then, barely suppressing the look that accompanied her surge of exultation did Kelly turn toward her audience.

A slow, approving smile crossed Gary's bronzed features. Good pupil. Learned fast, his thought addressed half to his horse.

This unique, thoroughly adorable and irreplaceable girl is indeed a woman for all the seasons, and you, Gary

Kelly's Quest

Hunnicutt, are the luckiest cowboy who ever saddled a horse. Now spend the rest of your life trying to deserve her.

Dancer, a very understanding horse nodded vigorously and nickered agreement.

With no perceptible motion, a smile of well-being on his handsome face, Gary pressed the "go ahead button" on Dancer and loped easily toward Kelly.

Freeze Frame

Buddy Ebsen

About the Author

Buddy Ebsen's best known characterization is that of "Jed Clampett" patriarch of that celebrated piece of Americana *The Beverly Hillbillies*. His second best known is the television sleuth *Barnaby Jones*.

Prior to that he was "Georgie Russell," Davy's pal in the Walt Disney classic *Davy Crockett*.

Surprisingly, Buddy had never intended to be an actor. His goal in life was to be a doctor. However, after completing two years of pre-med studies at the University of Florida and Rollins College, the Florida land boom collapsed, affecting the fortunes of the Ebsen family.

Since Ebsen senior was a dancing teacher, he had taught all his children his trade. Buddy shuffled off to New York to try show business, arriving there August 4, 1928. His Broadway credits include: *Whoopee* 1928, *Flying Colors* 1933, *Ziegfeld Follies* 1934, *Yokel Boy* 1939, *Showboat* 1945 and *Male Animal* 1953.

His film credits include: *Broadway Melody of 1935* with his dancing partner, sister Vilma, *Broadway Melody of 1938* with Judy Garland, *Born to Dance*, the Shirley Temple picture *Captain January*, *Banjo On My Knee*, *Girl of the Golden West* 1938, *Parachute Battalion*, *Night People* with Gregory Peck 1954, *Between Heaven & Hell* 1956 with Robert Wagner, *Attack*, *Breakfast at Tiffany's* with Audrey Hepburn 1961, *Mail Order Bride* 1964, *The One & Only*

Family Band 1968, *The President's Plane is Missing, Fire on the Mountain* 1981, *Stone Fox* 1986, to name a few.

His creation of *Cabaret Dada*, a musical was inspired by the Dada artistic revolt as a protest against World War I. A song from that show was selected for world-wide broadcasting in seven languages by the Voice of America. In 1968, he won the Honolulu race in his thirty-five foot catamaran, "Polynesian Concept."

Buddy had painting lessons as a child, but this introduction to art did not flower until his later years. From casual pen and ink sketches of old Duke and Uncle Jed he was encouraged by his wife, Dorothy, herself a painter, to try oil.

This led to a brisk sale of originals and three limited edition serigraphs of 300 each, *Hong Kong, Sea Power*, and *Sedona* presently ninety percent sold out. *The Uncle Jed Country* limited edition series of ten paintings represent a return to, and the development of, his original inspiration Jed Clampett and Old Duke.